PASSING THE BATON

Jean Helen Ramm

Pen Press

© Jean Helen Ramm 2012

All rights reserved

No part of this publication may be reproduced, stored in a retrieval system, or transmitted in any form or by any means, without the prior permission in writing of the publisher, nor be otherwise circulated in any form of binding or cover other than that in which it is published and without a similar condition including this condition being imposed on the subsequent purchaser.

First published in Great Britain by Pen Press

All paper used in the printing of this book has been made from wood grown in managed, sustainable forests.

ISBN 978-1-78003-453-9

Printed and bound in the UK
Pen Press is an imprint of
Indepenpress Publishing Limited
25 Eastern Place
Brighton
BN2 1GJ

A catalogue record of this book is available from the British Library

Cover design by Jacqueline Abromeit

My thanks to Dave, Gillian and my artist friends at Eltham Leisure Centre... and with apologies to Bird and Fortune who are always with me at dinner parties.

Contents

Go Baby, Go	1
Dinner Party: One	15
Come Winter, Come Spring	18
Snack Lunch: Saturday	43
Come Fly With Me	45
Breakfast: Saturday	56
Dirty Water	58
Breakfast: Sunday	71
Dreams And Drives	74
Dinner Party: Two	92
Fly Me To The Moon	95
About the author	109

Go Baby, Go

He drove out of the tunnel alongside a cluster of heavy lorries careering towards the continent. On south-east London soil now, and momentarily the sun shone cheerfully on his home patch. His birthplace. To his left, the area that had been contaminated and then reborn. Reinvented. The colours and designs of the new structures sitting awkwardly with the old. Eventually time and trees would help. His mood was gloomy. He told himself to cheer up, put a smile on like you had to do at work sometimes when you really felt like blowing the place up. Soon he was off the main road and heading for Woolwich and Plumstead Common. He warned himself to adjust his driving, he was no longer on the motorway, but his foot didn't relax its pressure on the accelerator.

When he screeched to a halt at red lights a group of slim Asian girls looked at him disparagingly from the pavement. Then they smiled quietly to each other as they crossed. As the lights turned orange, then green, three Western adolescent boys crossed nonchalantly in slow motion, just to make a point. He pipped smartly but they continued their snail-like pace. Two of them wore earrings and wide flapping trousers with low-hanging crutches. The third was in a tight lycra tracksuit which made his muscular legs and buttocks look like mounds of rising dough.

"Cheer up, cheer up." He said it aloud as he revved and drove off trying to feel the pleasure his car had brought him. His BMW. This year's model. A company car. 'Boy Done Good!' Now he was driving into familiar territory. Some things never changed. Plumstead Common had style. It was little changed from the days he used to play footy here as a child but when he tried to picture himself in those tight little shorts, Brenda's image kept coming into his head. Her neck and mouth mostly, but sometimes her eyes. Troubles. Troubles. What was he going to do about Brenda? He shouldn't be coming here. He needed to sort his own life out and then do this visit, but could it be sorted? He struggled to gather thoughts about his last visit to London but Brenda continued to dominate. Oh yes, their visit to Brisbane last year to see old friends and celebrate 25 years of marriage. The pleasure they'd shared in the surf. The way they'd laughed and fallen over together as the waves rolled in.

He swore to himself as he sped through red lights when he knew well that he had time to stop. Another vehicle hooted at him.

As he drew up outside the house, he could see his mother's head and shoulders down at basement level. Was she looking out for him? She shouted to him as he lifted his overnight bag out of the boot.

"He's no better. Y'father's no better…"

Neil opened his eyes wide and shook his head. The surf was rolling in and Brenda was sipping wine on a nearby terrace. Happy times.

His mother looked dishevelled, yet she was a woman who had always cared about her appearance. He wished he didn't have to see her like this. It was something he'd never anticipated and on first encounter it still shocked him. This morning she could have been a dirty old witch who was anxious to get back indoors to check her latest brew. He told himself to calm down. His parents needed to see him.

"Got me right on the ankles when I was standing at the sink… one of these days I'll take that stick off him."

There was never a greeting for him these days. She spoke to him as if he was there all the time, when in fact he lived with his wife and teenage children miles away in Yorkshire, and it was four months since his last visit. These days it was the same when he phoned, as if she thought he was there every day sitting on the settee with them, knowing their most intimate interactions. Omniscient.

"I'm not going to take it, Neil. I mean it this time."

Neil felt a stiffness in his knees, after four hours in the car. Awful hold-ups on the M11 as usual. He seemed to have arthritis creeping into his joints, which he tried to ignore, but at times like this his knees nearly let him down. His first reaction was always to laugh. It was easy to exaggerate these first signs of ageing. There was something inherently ridiculous about the human body as it started to slow down and fall apart. Visiting parents like this made good and bad vibes. If you were lucky it brought back some of the sparks of childhood tucked away somewhere inside but it also had a way of putting you in context on the ageing scale. Here you are, here they are, and there are your children, making their own lives now, making their own decisions. Choosing. Picking options. And recently the big shocker... giving options. 'Dad. We're off skiing to Austria at Xmas. You and Mum could join us... No don't say it... we thought you might not, but we'll all get together for a turkey lunch at New Year.' Fine. Fine. What a good thing for offspring to do. Exercise. Snow. The warm glow of après ski. New friends. Sister and brother on same trip. It should all gladden the heart.

He took a deep breath and leaned to kiss his mother on the cheek.

"You'll see what I mean. Watch what you say to him."

That conspiratorial tone. It hadn't taken long. She didn't seem to notice the kiss. The terrace house had three storeys with narrow curving steps outside down to the basement door, where they now stood. There were two broad steps up to the main front door on the first floor. His parents spent their days in the basement and never used the proper front door. His mother had put a curtain across it inside many years ago, complaining that the draught came through and it increased the heating bill. Yet they still went up to the top floor to sleep. Two steep flights of stairs. Both had suffered strokes and his father in particular had a debilitating weakness down his right side.

"The traffic was awful on the M11..."

In the old days she would have fussed and sympathised. He put his bag down, and wished he could leave. His mother's first remarks were, if anything, more discouraging than on his last visit. They were still at loggerheads. He couldn't get used to it. Didn't like it. Tried to forget each time he drove back North. Last time it had felt like walking into a bog which kept getting deeper and cloggier until in the end he couldn't move, either to get further in or out. Now he just wanted to get back into his car and put his foot down. He looked into the pale blue eyes of his mother. They were still fine eyes. It was her mouth that had changed, the victim of a gradual but relentless subsidence.

"I tell you, Neil. I won't answer for what I might do."

She was on that precipice between anger and tears.

"Mum. Calm down."

She barely heard him, so absorbed was she in her own feelings. She started to swear to herself in whispers.

"The bugger, the bugger, the bugger..."

Neil was startled. He'd never known her as bad as this before. So, sort of, uninhibited.

His father came into the room leaning heavily on his stick and breathing oddly, deliberately, as if his lungs were some kind of engine which took most of his time and attention. He'd had respiratory problems for years now. He nodded at his son but did not allow himself to be distracted from the engine.

"He hit me with his stick, Neil. Lashed out at my feet while I was at the sink."

Neil did not want to slip straight into a mediation role, especially not today. He needed the old times back when he gathered himself while they asked about his journey, their grandchildren, the BMW he was driving. He was their only child and he'd been brought up to 'do well,' 'to better himself,' and not to 'stick around here all your life.' He'd done all that. He'd managed it and more. Walking in like this, it was worse than he'd anticipated. Grumbles, yes. He had got used to that but they had more recently started to complain about each other which was not like them. Before that they had joked about old age and done things to support each other. Now all that had changed.

His father was sitting, listening, and looking at him, as if expecting to be rebuked. Neil looked down, not wanting eye contact with either parent, wanting only a few minutes alone with a cup of tea.

"How's Brenda?"

His mother. At last! A sign of the old interest and concern.

"She's okay."

"Brenda... Brenda..." His father this time, puzzling over the words or the image, it was impossible to know.

"Yes. She's fine. Still working at the same hotel and enjoying it. Thinking of starting a degree in management."

Well, she was fine, of course. That was true, and she was thinking of more study. All true. She was also tearing their marriage to shreds, day by day by day. Brenda was having an affair and he was feeling wretched, left out, let down, unsure what steps to take. He had known for two weeks.

"That's not a good idea. Age she is. Take that long to do a degree. Not something to start in your forties."

Well at least his mother's response was rational and more like her normal self. In the past she had scolded Brenda for trying to do too much. His mother had always been so clear about priorities. Housewife and mother first. Her little jobs had had to fit in, take second place. No dilemmas there. Brenda was a different type of person. Brenda was caught up in the dynamic business of wife, mother career... and... sex. She was flying like he had always encouraged but...

His mother's tone was determined and she was shaking her head.

"I'll go for him, Neil. I'll get him back."

She seemed set on provoking her husband.

"I'll get him."

Neil shuffled uneasily wanting his thoughts on Brenda to persist but his mother was vying for his attention in a way she never did in the past when she would listen and encourage, show pleasure at his successes and laugh with him about life's absurdities. He looked down at his overnight bag. He couldn't take this. She owed it to him to control herself better than this. She was ranting now, looking like a witch again. Funny though the way they had asked after Brenda first. Usually it was the grandchildren.

The state he was in over Brenda began to flood all over him and numb him to everything else. How could she be doing this to him. He was still feeling as if he'd been cracked open and crushed and he didn't know where he was going, where they were going. Like when he used nut crackers at Christmas as a kid. Often he smashed the shell, crushed the nut and trapped his fingers. Apparently Brenda's... he was a rock musician from Leeds. Neil's eyes wandered to his mother's ankles. There were nasty red marks like bruises on the outsides. His father sat alert, contained, watching.

Rubbing the back of one of his knees, Neil went to the kitchen and clicked on the jug. A cup of tea. Still rubbing his knee he noticed how cold it was in the kitchen. How bare. Times were when he came here and the smell of roasting dinner greeted him at the door, and they both hung on his words as he brought them up to date on his 'good', 'successful', life. His latest plans. He would try to explain to them the intricacies of his job, as he relished the rich brown gravy and the juicy roast potatoes.

Now he was wondering what Brenda was up to. She didn't know he was in London. Ought he to phone her at work. Usually they operated a 'no news is good news' but it wasn't usual. It wasn't usual at all... the times were... well... it was like he needed to use wartime strategy. Time for a change in tactics. Calmly he pressed the digits on his mobile. Her ansaphone greeted him. He thought the message was slightly different, the huskiness of her voice enhanced. He sniffed importantly to himself and opened the oven door. There was plenty of fat left in there from the roasts of long ago, but the oven was no longer in use. In fact, there were some boxes of biscuits in there, and a roll of tinfoil. His parents had frozen meals delivered by the Council and these were heated daily in the microwave.

It had turned out that Brenda hated cooking and he had taken it on more and more. He could cook delicious Indian curries, and standing there in the bleak little kitchen he felt a rush of pride in himself and his mood lightened. For a time when the children were young he even made bread. His mother had not been comfortable with his breakfast baguettes on one of her rare visits to Yorkshire. Whereas Brenda had seemed proud, his mother had been unusually lost for words and the next morning had asked for cereal only.

He went back to the living area with his tea. She was going upstairs. He could hear her banging her way up the second flight. Condensation was running down the living room window pane and he noticed for the first time how rotten the frame had become.

"Tea, Dad?"

There was no reply.

"How are you then, Dad?"

The answer was obvious. The stroke last year had left his father with speech difficulties as well as the right-sided weakness, and his lungs had been a problem for years. There was a long pause and when it came it was slurred, but there was no mistaking the anger.

"Tell that woman… I'm fighting fit."

"Da..ad," he rebuked. "Mum's the one person you really need."

Neil's eyes scanned the round rose-like flowers on the carpet, the photographs. His graduation, the kids' school photographs at different ages. His wedding. All milestones indicating normality. At the wedding Brenda's face was upturned towards his, suppliant, shy. The rock musician had a ponytail and shouted when he performed. Brenda said he 'challenged' the audience. Okay Brenda. Okay.

"There are them that'll take anything. You can't trust anybody."

Was his father pointing at him, his mother upstairs or the chair he was sitting on, or was he on about the burglary next door? Something about a new three-piece suite being removed while owners were in Corfu. He recalled his mother telling him on the phone. The locals had watched it being removed and loaded into the van, believing it was going back to the manufacturer because it was in some way faulty.

"You can't trust anybody, mate."

The statement echoed in his head.

"Dad. What are you talking about?"

The doorbell rang and his father began the process that would lead to him standing and walking, but it was not completed as his mother came banging down the stairs and let the person in, and his father flopped back into his seat.

"Hello Tony. How are you today?"

The woman spoke as she bustled cheerfully through to the kitchen. Did she wink at him as she passed? Neil wasn't sure.

"Who's this, Dad?"

"Never seen that one before." His father was looking towards the kitchen.

"What rubbish you talk. You know she's from homecare." His mother sat down heavily. "They have a roster, Neil. Different ones, different days."

Now she was speaking with a bit more awareness, trying to explain.

"Silly... cows."

His father was looking at him for support.

Neil finished his tea. What was happening to the man who had always had respect for women and had told him as a young man 'They know what they're doing, son. In so many ways they've got more sense than us.' He got up and went through to the kitchen and out into the back garden, hardly acknowledging the woman who was putting food into the microwave. The garden was small and wild, the winter jasmine was blooming clear and yellow, claiming more space each time he came, and there was the honeysuckle, when in season, spreading rampantly down the boundary wall. In the old days the lawn had been like a carpet, level and spruce as the floors inside and clipped neatly around the edges. Dahlias and more dahlias were cultivated every year. Now huge nettles, drab and threatening, dominated the lawn and plastic bags fluttered around at the far end.

The cheerful woman came out to him at the back and said she was worried about his parents. She didn't think they were coping. She spoke with a strong local accent.

"Can't you and the family get together on it. Get it sorted?" Her tone was friendly.

"I am the family."

She looked at Neil and saw a man in a good suit. Expensive car. Only son. Only child. All the privileges.

"I am the family."

He repeated it as if she had no right to be asking. She tightened her mouth and went on to ask why he wasn't doing something to change the situation about his parents. Yes his mother was provocative but lately his father well, the authorities would call it physical abuse. She hesitated over the words 'physical abuse' and lowered the tone of her voice.

The more she talked the more he distanced himself and felt uninvolved. He knew she wanted to engage him but he stubbornly resisted and continued to look around the garden, adding casually, "After all these years. A bit of argument is to be expected."

"Yes but what I'm saying is it's more than that. It's not just, as you say 'a bit of argument'."

He had an urge to go back inside, pick up his overnight bag and put it back in the car. Instead a bell went 'ting' and she went back into the kitchen. He looked hard at the bright yellow jasmine flowers. So small, so fresh and perky. Her job was to heat their meals, and mind her own business. Her head appeared again briefly out the backdoor. He heard her saying.

"I have to warn you… It's my responsibility…" And then he heard "…Social Services and Police."

He stared at the nettles. For the first time he found himself thinking about his parents the same way he used to think about his kids on school open evenings – trying but not too hard, to be objective, mistrusting a lot that was being said, except this was sort of the other way round. Reports on his children at school were always suspiciously good.

When he went back in the woman had gone and his parents were tucking into their heated meals of chicken and rice with a bread pudding waiting on the sideboard. Food had brought a truce-like calm between them.

"Do you need any shopping, Mum?" He desperately wanted to do something but didn't know what. Certainly wasn't going upstairs with his overnight bag. His mother refused his offer, saying that the homecare collected the pension and did the shopping.

"I'll pop out and see if I can get you something a bit different."

"Please yourself."

*

At the corner shop the Indian woman behind the counter called out to her son to check the price of ham. He bought a newspaper, some bananas, a bunch of flowers and a quarter pound of the best honey roast ham. He was distracted by the woman's beautiful face. She took the money and didn't give him a bag until he asked. Her sari was a blaze of orange and sky blue. She seemed cross.

As he walked away from the shop he checked his mobile. Message from Brenda in capitals. CAN'T WAIT

TO SEE YOU. AM COOKING STEAK TONIGHT. Of course, he hadn't told her he was coming here. He had walked out in a huff and hadn't mentioned he was taking two days off work. So what did all this mean. She didn't usually send messages like this when he was at work. A kind of calm flooded over him but then the doubts crept back.

Back at the house he heard himself saying that something had cropped up at work and he had to get out of London before the rush. They accepted it without comment. In some respects he thought they were probably under the impression that he had been there overnight. His mother came out to the car with him and stood on the pavement as he loaded his bag.

"Next thing he'll be wanting sex."

He sort of heard but somehow refused proper access to her words and did not reply. He drove off up the road thinking only of getting back to Yorkshire and approached the tunnel glancing fleetingly across the peninsula to the Dome. He wanted to be home to his village on the right side of Leeds, his office in town, his own kitchen, and the rugs from Istanbul which Brenda had bought ten years ago. He was going there fast. No time to waste.

Brenda. But Brenda and this man. This man with a pony tail who provoked his audience. She has to let go of either him or me. She simply has to, has to, has to. Pony tail or not he was just another chap, a fact she had to realise. If she could shake off the erotic urges, see them as such. He wanted to stop the car and put his head down on the steering wheel, but instead he put his foot down on the accelerator. He sped by half a dozen heavy vehicles, revelling in the way his car held the road, took the bend in the tunnel. It was outrageous how he had let the matter drift. And it wasn't going to be all right with his parents either. Something had to happen, be done. His mother's ankles were purple. They had been hit hard.

'Sometimes drifting is a good thing.' Brenda's voice, eyes wide, a hint of appeal, begging to be able to carry on her intimacies. Just once more. Twice perhaps. 'I need time, Neil, to finish it properly.' Oh no my love. Not any more. Not any longer. No more time. Yes, we'll dine tonight on steak and sip our wine but you will make your decision. One or the other. Black is black, white is white. Grey is good but not in this situation.

As he roared out of the tunnel, heading for the M11, he began to feel clearer about himself. He would take a stand. He was 'Boy Done Good.' He grimaced. Today the term didn't amuse him but he really had… done good. Brenda had to face facts, but would she? He was the one who had to take a risk and draw a line. His parents were getting themselves into strife, no doubt about that, but he would deal with Brenda first. Get it sorted. Sort Brenda. That couldn't wait. He was a business man. He knew about priorities.

Beside him the traffic raged on all sides. At the last moment, he decided against the M11 and swung over to the right causing a series of vehicles to brake sharply behind him. Someone tooted at him, and his response was to increase his speed. Accelerate out of trouble. That was the way to do it. No good slowing down and making courteous gestures to other drivers. Go for it. If you didn't look after yourself, nobody else would. Now he was on the anti-clockwise route of the North Circular, in the fast lane, overtaking massive lorries with a white-haired man in an open-topped sports car in the middle lane seeming to be trying to get ahead of him. Then he was on the A1 and it was only fifteen minutes later that he noted a massive traffic jam ahead. Too late now to go back or turn off. He put the radio on and loud rock music emanated from the speakers. Who gave them the go-ahead to shout their mouths off like this? Bastards. He was in the fast lane, overtaking two lanes of stationary traffic. No doubt further ahead this lane would be closed, but that wouldn't deter him, he'd force himself in on the left. You had to be assertive in life, not just stay in line.

Then somehow his concentration wavered. He was high on speed. The rock music was blaring out now, the singer in his prime, rhythms backing his defiance. In his head he was home, facing Brenda across a candlelit dining table. He never knew that his car somersaulted and landed in a fragmented mess, never heard the sirens and was unaware of the dead body lifted skilfully into the ambulance.

Meanwhile, his mother was making her way upstairs for her afternoon nap and his father had put the racing on TV but couldn't recall whether he'd put a bet on. He hadn't, of course.

Dinner Party: One

All: Cheers…

CLINK OF GLASSES

Susan: It was a great sight, Cyril. School sports. Our son ran last… I mean, not last… well, last leg of the relay race.

Kathy: Very important place … hmmm nice champagne.

Susan: It was so exciting. Their team was running in second place up to the final baton change… tell them, Tom, I need to check something in the kitchen.

Tom: …and would you believe the front runners messed up the baton change… and Jake raced ahead.

Kathy: Oh really! How exciting!

Tom: My darling wife was so proud… come along let's move to the table now and get started.

Cyril: Yes. Bring it on. Red please, Tom. Yes the Cotes de Rhone… thanks.

Tom: Well it's made me think, we're all in a relay. You can say that about so many things.

Cyril: You mean like rugby?

Tom: Yes many games but also politics. You can pass the baton in all kinds of ways.

Kathy: Oh yes. Pass the blame you mean.

Tom: Exactly Cyril.

Kathy: Meanwhile… er… could you pass the bowl, careful. Don't drop it!

SHRIEKS OF LAUGHTER

Kathy: I just love avocado in salad. Cyril and I are in favour of Cameron's big society. Wonderful idea. More to be done by families, neighbours, voluntary groups, charities…

Susan: Hmm… sounds great.

Cyril: I mean that's what you've got to have… like the old days… the right attitude, people wanting to help. All about 'getting together'.

Tom: That's what we need, Cyril.

Susan: But, what about the many serious social problems. They can't be solved just by 'getting together.'

Cyril: 'Getting together' that's the answer, Susan… yes just a touch more red, thanks. Do you belong any community groups?

Susan: No. No. We're either working or over at our place in France. Lovely food in that small town isn't it, Tom… tell them…

Tom: Oh yes. Their moules and frites… wow! But Cyril, we can't do everything… prisons, mental health…

Cyril: Mental patients. Don't mention them. We've just had a place opened near us. Is this wine New World?

Tom: Problem is it?

Cyril: Which, Tom, the mad house or the New World?

Tom: Could be both, mate.

Cyril: Patients sometimes wander out into the street looking as if they're sleepwalking. Never know what they might do. Hmmm… good smell… Cheers… this is a good one. I wouldn't want to go in there encouraging them to play tennis and make cup cakes.

Tom: Hey Cyril, cheers. That's it then they can't pass the baton to us.

Cyril: No. We'll drop it, Tom.

Tom: And run?

Cyril: Yes. Like the devil.

Tom: Hmm… like a bat-on out of hell.

SHRIEKS OF LAUGHTER

Come Winter, Come Spring

The sun shone through the French windows onto his newspaper. He was sitting in the centre of the brightest patch, in an easy chair, allowing himself a few relaxed moments. The cat snuggled up beside him on the chair, seeming affectionate but in fact awaiting the opportunity to take over the warm, sun-filled spot which he now occupied. He glanced across at his wife. She was small and slender with delicate shoulders and badly decaying teeth. She needed a dental appointment. Her hair shone, dark, with a burnished glow, falling across her face now as she settled into the settee.

A plane flew overhead. He imagined the pilot making adjustments to land, telling the passengers the sun was shining on this green and pleasant land. They had been attracted to this house because of its proximity to the airport, thinking of all the places they could so easily visit from here.

"Doesn't Sonya stay for Art Club today?"

He spoke after what had been hours of silence between them, and watching her now, he did not expect a reply. It wasn't unusual these days for him to speak to her like this when there was some doubt as to her level of consciousness. He was used to his own questions resounding around the room. He felt they were struggling in a fog, hanging on, hoping to somehow emerge into gentle sunshine. They had been there in the sunlight. They really had, but so long ago.

"No. It finished last week. The Art Club."

She had heard and responded. Slowly, but a response. He felt just a tiny lightening movement in his head, a far cry from optimism, more a gladdening movement, a flutter. Her words were a bit slurred, but what she said would be right. The children. Their activities. She clung on to these details, even in a semiconscious state when nothing else she said made sense. She was half standing now, tottering, restless, as she reached for extra cushions, then resettling and lifting her legs onto the settee, without removing her shoes.

He finished the article he was reading about a famous footballer having a vasectomy. That was something he had planned for himself. They had talked about it, in the old days, the days of gentle sunlight. The two girls made their family complete. No more children needed. Now it was all irrelevant. They never did all those pleasurable things that resulted in pregnancy. The way they were now there would certainly not be anymore children anyway.

Before he had reached for his coat and the house keys she was breathing deeply. Checking the fridge he saw that she had taken the children's prepared meals out of the freezer ready to be heated for this evening. Lamb stewed with onions and paprika and 'retes' with cherries and ice cream. Two little containers of each course. A roster was pinned over the freezer. Tomorrow it would be 'gulyas' and the next day 'paprikas osirke'.

He headed for the school, walking very straight, like a soldier, marching almost, eyes straight ahead. Times like today he didn't think he would ever get used to living in a London suburb with what he regarded as fields and fields of semidetached houses mingling with council blocks, and trees standing graciously, their roots penetrating the earth below concrete and tarmac. Urbanised trees. He was sure they suffered, but they were magnificent. To him living like this, in such close proximity to other people, often seemed bizarre. All the privacy, all the emotion that made up a single household, all focussed within the bricks and mortar of houses with sometimes only a single wall or a worn-out fence dividing them. So close, yet so separate and so contained.

Other parents were beginning to cluster around the school gates, and stalling for time he went into the nearby shop. The Turkish newsagent looked at him with interest as he sold him cigarettes and watched him light up outside the door. This customer was not like the others. You could tell he didn't come from round here. He wasn't one of the locals. Funny. He always wore those shiny shoes with his anorak, and that kind of beard was way out of fashion for a Western man, but his daughters seemed so fond of him, so co-operative, unlike many others round here, when their parent asked them not to touch things in his shop.

"Daddy. Daddy. Can Michelle come home to play?" His youngest daughter danced up to him holding the hand of a tiny girl with glasses.

"Not today, Lisette, Mummy isn't well."

There was always an excuse, but Lisette never gave up. Michelle turned away, delighted to have been invited and not in the least perturbed by the rejection. Her mother gave Frank a quick glance as she hustled her daughter into the car. Sometimes he got the impression that he was regarded with suspicion, and these days he wasn't making any effort to talk to other parents.

"When will you come to get us in our car, Dad?" asked Sonya, his eldest, as they made their way towards home. "Rachel's mother is going to start meeting her in a car every day, and Rachel's my best friend."

Frank hesitated. His lovely Mondeo was unused, unregistered, not roadworthy, and had been so for at least a year now.

"You're putting it right, aren't you, Dad. Making it go. It won't always and always be in the garage." She didn't want an answer, she was making a statement as she skipped beside him.

The garage had become his area, where he went every evening. He was working on it alright. He had a heater in there and the car bonnet had been up for weeks. His place. Now he was thinking how typical it was of Eleni these days that she had no idea to what extent the garage was his refuge. It never occurred to her to walk down the garden, open the door and have a good look round inside. Surely that was what wives normally did. Probed. Pried. Checked. Encouraged. In the old days even in winter she used to sit in the car and talk to him as he worked on the engine, before shivering back indoors and reappearing with two mugs of tea. Now she just didn't seem to care, although somewhere along the line it had started to be said that when the car was on the road again they would all go to see grandmother in Hungary. He wasn't sure how this assumption had developed. He had not had the car out of their local area except for a couple of trips to his home county and that was ages ago.

It wasn't going well, his project in the garage. Apart from unidentified problems with the engine, there was something seriously wrong with the Ford's electrics and he'd tried to work rigorously to a book on car maintenance which had a whole section on electricity. Only on one occasion, six months or so ago, did he have grounds for optimism when there was an encouraging cough and the engine shuddered into action, but it was short-lived. There followed a juddering motion and then silence.

Back indoors with the children he went into the after school routine. Careful hanging up on the hall pegs of school coats and bags. Orange or apple juice? Change school clothes for jeans and T-shirts. Slippers out from the hall cupboard. Shoes cleaned for tomorrow.

"Daddy, can we put our trainers on?"

Sonya wasn't sure she wanted to be indoors for the rest of the evening.

"Daddy, we love watching the planes outside."

"Well, you're not going out again today."

"But Mummy said we had to get exercise after school. You did, didn't you, Mummy?"

Sonya ran into the lounge and gave a grown-up little "Oh" sound as she looked at her mother on the settee.

"Never mind, we'll wear our slippers, Ettie, and keep our trainers for Saturday."

Sonya spoke authoritatively and Lisette looked at her trustingly and eagerly complied before running into the kitchen for her apple juice, happily wearing her slippers. Frank looked down at their dancing feet. Slippers or trainers? It was a big decision. Slippers meant they were confined to the inside. They all understood that. That had to be clear. If they were outside at the back, he needed to know.

"Sonya. Get your homework out now."

He liked everything to do with objects to be methodical. At the moment this suited Sonya. She took pleasure in her homework. Now she went importantly to her school bag on its peg in the hall, took out the homework, placed it on the table near the French window, and replaced the bag. Lisette looked on, impressed. She didn't have homework yet.

Frank watched as Sonya started to write short sentences in a tiny exercise book. "As soon as you've finished, I'll put the telly on."

"Daddy, can I have it on now. I won't listen." Lisette meant 'with the sound turned right down'.

"No, Lisette. We'll wait for Sonya."

Lisette got up and walked over to her mother, carrying her juice. She stared for a few seconds at the unconscious heap and then turned away.

"Sonya. Can I do some writing?" Sonya obliged by tearing out the last page of her exercise book and handing it to her sister with a pencil. For fifteen minutes the children were absorbed in their activities, and when Sonya said, "Finished" and closed her book with a flourish, Frank switched on the television, and the sisters sat together on the floor.

Sonya cast the briefest of glances at her mother, still slumped on the settee, wearing that green jumper, 'Kermit green,' that's what it was, and it used to make them all laugh. Her mother had said it first. Today Sonya didn't mention it, she just looked at her mother's slim legs in their badly laddered tights. Why didn't she go upstairs and lie on the bed. The settee was where she and Ettie most liked to be after school. They liked having half the settee each and arguing over the cushions while their mother was in the kitchen heating their food.

"Daddy. Look at Mummy's tights. Look Ettie!"

Her younger sister looked, her face a mixture of seriousness and amusement. She didn't care about the state of her mother's tights, she was fed up with her mother. It wasn't fair, Michelle not being able to come to play. She had only been to play once. Although, it wasn't nice being ill either. She didn't want her mother ill. Lisette remembered being ill herself when she'd had those nightmares, and her mother had sat beside her bed for ages, night after night, telling her it wasn't real, that she was not really in a dark forest with wolves lurking behind trees inviting her to share their picnic and telling her that they had eaten her grandmother.

"They're only ladders, silly."

Sonya responded vaguely, concentrating now on the screen. Lisette started to laugh. She had never seen so many ladders in her mother's tights, and underneath on one leg the skin was all red, you could see it through the ladders.

"Why are they called ladders?"

Sonya didn't want to talk anymore.

"Ask Daddy."

Lisette looked towards her father in the kitchen and started to smile to herself as she caught sight of him in the heavy plastic pinafore. He looked really funny in it because it had flowers all over and 'Welcome to Hungary' in the Hungarian language. Grandmother had sent it from Budapest. Their mother looked even funnier in it as it was so large and she was so small. Sometimes Sonya put it on and it trailed on the floor.

Frank was checking the cooking times which were written clearly in Eleni's handwriting on a list beside the breadbin. He brought the food out onto the table, and while they ate the television was turned off and he sat with them at the table. Today he reread some of the Daily Mail and noticed with relief that Lisette was looking tired. Bed fairly early, hopefully. Eleni hated the Daily Mail, calling it a 'common paper.' Sometimes she came in with the Guardian, but she didn't read for long. These days she couldn't concentrate.

He went out to make sure the heater was on in the garage. In fact it had been on since last night and the place was cosy. He scolded himself. He must remember to turn it off. Everything else was there. He checked his watch. Two hours and the kids would be up in their bedroom. He relished for a moment the familiarity, the 'garagey' smell, the drone of aircraft coming in to land, the sight of the green Mondeo, C registration, waiting patiently with the engine revealed. He turned the heater right down and returned to the kitchen. He washed up, put the newspaper in the dustbin and gave the girls a few sweets.

When Sonya eventually followed her sister upstairs to prepare for bed, it was his sign to go out to the garage. Now he found himself looking at Eleni and trying to control a surge of fury which engulfed him and then seeped away as he continued to look at her and remember. What was she doing? A mother with such aspirations, such a passionate belief in education, books and the better life waiting there, to be reached for, to be claimed. How she had impressed and inspired him. And here she lay like a drunken tramp. 'Oh I only drink wine. I love a glass when the children have gone to bed.' That was Eleni in the past. Frighteningly he thought she still believed this.

He allowed himself now to go over the social worker's visit two weeks ago. Exactly two weeks today. He had kept his distance at first, and let Eleni deal with the woman.

Fortunately Eleni had just returned from taking the children to school and she was sober. Mornings were her good time.

He'd listened from the hall but then the social worker had asked him to be part of the discussion, and once they were all seated the woman had looked carefully at them both, saying, "I must be straight with you. This is an investigation. A child protection investigation."

The voice was serious, the words well-articulated, practised. He had felt shock go through him like a bullet but Eleni had been unruffled.

"I'm here because the headteacher of your children's school has reported that you were so inebriated... well that was her word 'inebriated', Mrs Barnes... that you, you fell over at the school gate... Wednesday last week... er..." The voice faltered, the social worker looked down at her notes.

Eleni interrupted. "That is not right. I didn't collect them on Wednesday. My husband did."

"Well it may have been Thursday, but it has been reported... as I say... that you fell over at the gates."

Frank waited. How would his wife deal with this?

"It seems that you have not got your facts right." Eleni spoke with a quiet dignity. "First you say Wednesday, now Thursday, and, in any case, it is nobody's business if I fell over at the school gates, except to help me get up. I do not understand your questions."

She looked critically at the social worker, who continued, "And I'm afraid the Head's report states that this has happened before."

Eleni looked at Frank.

"This is awful. I cannot believe it. All those children out there needing protection and you come to us."

Eleni's voice was controlled, her slim shoulders looked gaunt as she changed her position on the settee. Frank would like to have told the social worker to leave, but intuition told him that would make things worse. He was guarded and silent, but inside he was exclaiming at his wife's composure. He stared at the fine, silky strands of hair which Eleni kept pushing behind her ear. He saw how attractive she was. Intelligent. She gave a little laugh.

"My children are the most special things… the most precious thing in my life. Their care… their future… it is always with me."

"But do you have another explanation for your falls?" The social worker was trying to bring together the headteacher's report and this apparently sensitive, caring woman seated before her. There was silence and she repeated herself.

"Falling outside the school. The information I have says it has happened more than once. Do you have another explanation?"

"It has been frosty, slippery. And you aren't always well are you, Eleni?"

Frank blurted this out and Eleni spoke before he had finished. "I have some kind of spinal problem which affects my gait."

The social worker shook her head and made a note on her pad. This case wasn't going to reach crisis point today, she had decided that already. There was no direct route to fostering these children in spite of the pressure from the school. She couldn't help liking this woman, but that was not important. In the end, when decisions had to be made, like or dislike was irrelevant.

Eleni began to talk about her visits to the GP, and how unhelpful he had been, and her plans to consult a doctor in Budapest where her mother lived. The social worker was quick to draw Eleni out further on the subject of the grandmother, and Eleni talked on about their plans to drive across Europe for a family visit, and the time two years ago when she had flown out with the children. She took the woman into the kitchen to show her all the nutritious little meals in their tinfoil containers in the freezer, stressing her belief and pleasure in preparing healthy Hungarian food, which had been the dishes she had enjoyed as a child. Frank did not add further to the conversation in the kitchen except to nod in support of his wife's explanations. His guardedness continued. He'd had little to do with the authorities but he read newspapers and knew social workers might seem bland but they could be dangerous.

Then, as the conversation in the kitchen appeared to be reaching a natural conclusion, the social worker asked for a drink of water and suggested they all sit back in the lounge. She started to say positive things about what she had just seen for instance of the food preparations and the general care of the girls, and then asked how long they had known each other. Frank began to relax more and found he was willing to join in, describing his first meeting with Eleni on Waterloo Station in the coffee bar where she worked. His train had been delayed because of a strike, and within a year they had married and managed to put a deposit on their house.

They chatted for half an hour, the conversation dipping and diving around the personal aspects of both their lives, including Eleni's reasons for leaving Budapest, and the eventual arrival of the children. The social worker left saying that she would have to do another visit in about two weeks' time, and that she would have to report back to the school, see the children and speak to the GP. Strangely, he felt better immediately after she left, as if the talking and the explaining, and the being listened to, had brought something more alive into the atmosphere.

Remembering all this, as he now looked down at his wife, he acknowledged bitterly to himself how soon the silences had returned. He felt the fog again, not only restricting his vision, but making him dull, incapable of change and movement.

"What if the social worker had turned up today?"

He said it aloud, very slowly and deliberately, and the words hung in the air for a few seconds, but he did not expect a response.

"Eleni. Any time now, that social worker could be knocking at the door. She said two weeks."

She looked pathetic. What sort of a mother was she? He wanted to spit.

"I leave it to you, Eleni, because I'm going to the garage."

He went upstairs to check the girls, and then slipped quietly out of the back door.

*

When she came round it was daylight. The mantelpiece clock said four thirty but she reminded herself that these days it always said that time. She listened for the sound of the children, their voices and the dull clump of their feet upstairs. Nothing. When she sat up and tried to stand, her joints were stiff and her chest felt tight. She reached for her watch. Nine thirty. She went to look at the hooks in the hall. Nothing there, just the hooks. So it was morning. He would have taken them to school again but it should have been her this morning. She went to check the cupboard under the stairs. Yes. He had remembered it was PE for Sonya. Her kit wasn't there. Eleni rubbed her back. She thought again that there was something wrong with her spine. If she tried to stretch it hurt, and it had been like this for months. On her last visit the GP had refused to give her medication and had recommended more exercise, which was no help at all. She told herself that she would go to a doctor in Budapest, perhaps this summer.

She went through to the kitchen and checked the freezer. Ten twenty now and still no sign of Frank. There was only one more week's supply of prepared food left. Soon she would have to cook another batch. This time she was going to do more of the paprika chicken with tiny dumplings and the 'halaszle'. They loved soup. She had made notes about this and checked the notebook was still in the kitchen drawer. She wrote eggs on the shopping list. Her hand was shaking. Frank would only have free-range and she agreed with him. He had grown up on a smallholding in Devon, and couldn't abide the idea of chickens never allowed out to peck freely in the ground. Once, years ago, when the car was in use, and before the children, he had driven her to Devon. No one left in his family. Parents dead. He an only child. The gentle slopes and the colours of green and burnished gold had stayed in her head. Prior to this, London had been her only experience of England. They had gone again when the children were little. It had snowed on their way back to London. The children's excitement inside the car with the large flakes floating across the window made her smile now as she searched for her purse, eventually finding it in her bag underneath the cushions on the settee.

She had to go to the Post Office. She started to look for her lipstick. He wouldn't be pleased. She usually took the girls in the morning. Mornings were supposed to be when she was in charge. She tried to retrieve the image of snow falling softly around a slowly moving car, and the sounds little children make when they are delighted. No. It wouldn't come back Instead her head was full of images of Frank in his postman's uniform standing in the hall, phoning his boss, asking for more sick leave, and his eyes looking at her in anger and alarm. She went back to the notebook, to check if she had put eggs on the list. She thought she was no good at practical matters. Ideas were her thing. Literature. Art. The English language which she had studied so thoroughly at University. Everything now was such an effort. Just day by day, by day, by day. No proper beginning and end to anything. It was as if she and Frank were injured, or as if they were running in a three-legged race, and everyone else around them was without handicap. They were slipping further and further behind moving in awkward, jerky strides, holding each other back. Struggling. Unsure of the finishing line.

She imagined him leaving the children this morning at the school gates, and thought again of Sonya's PE kit. She checked again, but it wasn't in the cupboard. Good sign but where was he? Should be home by now.

*

In fact after leaving the children at school he had made himself walk. He was a postman. He needed to be a good walker. He had gone over to the common and stepped out methodically, forcing himself, checking his watch every few minutes to make sure he was going at the right pace. As a postman he had been efficient and punctual. He aimed at walking three and a half miles an hour but that was a bit fast for him. Today he spent a lot of time thinking about how to build up his speed. This morning he felt absolutely exhausted. A familiar feeling.

Back at the house he met her at the front door. She would be going to the Post Office shop. These days that was the only time she put lipstick on. The fact that her teeth were not brushed, and her coat was stained and creased made no impact. He saw only the lipstick and thought 'Child Benefit'. He watched her go slowly and deliberately across the road. How despicable she was, and yet, as well, such a lovely person, so still on the settee when he had left this morning. But it was she who was supposed to take the children in the morning. He often collected, but she had to take them. His sick leave would run out and then where would they be? Her translation work had somehow ceased to happen.

He went down to the garage and fiddled with the heater. It needed a new wick and he noticed he would soon be out of paraffin. He must not settle in there at this time of day. He forced himself to return indoors. These days he was going too often to the garage on the pretext of checking the heater. He reminded himself that once, early evening, would be sufficient.

He knew what was in the plastic bag when she returned. He heard the chink of bottle against bottle. Deep down inside him a voice started to laugh hysterically as he challenged her.

"Eleni. You're overdoing it."

What an understatement. He despaired at his choice of words. She looked at him and his patience snapped.

"The sherry. The booze! For Christ's sake woman."

Now it was the voice he disliked, loud and rough, like his father used to speak to the cows when they wouldn't go into their proper stalls.

"We soon need more shopping."

She was pretending not to hear him and referring to the children's meal plan. He struggled to control himself. The cat walked out from the lounge, across the hall where they were standing and up the stairs, where normally she wasn't allowed.

"You're deceiving yourself woman, you're having yourself on," his voice was still rough but he couldn't stop now.

"Having yourself on?"

She looked at him enquiringly. Her English was good but occasionally her comprehension let her down.

"Oh don't give me that. Kidding yourself. Kidding yourself, woman. Why are you buying sherry at this time in the morning? Don't think I can't see."

"Kidding? I'm not kidding myself, Frank. Some of my recipes—"

He gave a loud howl, "Your recipes! Your recipes are fine. It's you... you stupid fucking woman."

She didn't react outwardly to the swearing but he knew his words had hit home.

"If you could get a better job, Frank."

Frank gritted his teeth and closed his lips tight. There they were again. Fighting in the fog. Lashing out at each other. Hitting home. She could always turn it like this, quietly, innocently almost, back onto him. And then again, Frank felt that she was, in some respects, right. Absolutely right. He went blindly out of the back door, standing for a moment on the small patch of overgrown lawn trying to dispel his anger. He could see her moving around in the kitchen. They had to stop all this but they had gone too far. They were lurching dangerously from one act to another. The thing that bound them together was hurting, pulling at them, imprisoning them. Then he went back indoors and found she was opening one of the bottles of sherry. He wanted to smash it on her head but he didn't. He held her shoulders and kicked her hard on her right shin. She took it with a sharp intake of breath and a long groan and her grip on the bottle tightened. He turned and retraced his steps out of the back door.

*

Eleni sat for a while in the sun beside the French window rubbing her bruised shin, feeling no anger, only shame. She got up and managed to put some of the children's clothes into the washing machine, and took some time to set up the ironing board, trapping her fingers badly. She tried to concentrate on ironing two school blouses, becoming totally preoccupied, now and again burning herself as she tried to press the tiny collars. This blouse of Sonya's was too small for her, but it was still in good condition. She was pressing the iron on the pocket, thinking of Lisette and how she would like to have her sister's blouse. It wouldn't always be like this, of course, the time would soon come when Lisette would not want her sister's cast-offs.

The phone rang and she thought it might be her mother in Budapest asking how the car repairs were going, but it was the social worker making an appointment to come if possible tomorrow.

"There are some really important things to talk over."

Eleni agreed saying it must be in the morning as in the afternoon she might be busy with translation work. As she replaced the receiver and reached for the calendar in the kitchen where she kept dates related to her children, she smelt burning. The iron. She turned it off, lifting it from the pocket of Sonya's blouse. It was more than a scorch. The blouse was ruined. She thought miserably of Frank, and started to rub her leg. It hurt and she could see it was bruised through the ladders in her tights. This was the second time he had done that…

She stared for some time at the burn mark on Sonya's blouse, and then poured herself a large sherry and sat down in an easy chair. A plane hovered overhead and she thought of how good it would be to fly to Budapest. Perhaps one day. It was thanks to her dead uncle's will that they had managed to put a deposit on this house. All that had coincided with meeting Frank for the first time at Waterloo Station where she was working in a restaurant. He had been downhearted. His father's farm taken over by debtors. She had another sip of sherry and got up to put the scorched blouse in a bag and then into the rubbish bin. Gradually morning slipped into noon and life seemed bearable and blurred. Frank must be in the garage working on the car. She refilled her glass with water. Her mouth was dry. It felt like it was lined with sandpaper.

She had a short doze and woke in a blurred state of panic. Ah, it was okay. Not time for the children and anyway Frank was doing it today. He did the pick-ups... except ah, today, oh yes, he had taken them this morning. She hadn't even done her bit. Perhaps this afternoon she'd do it. She looked out of the back door, beginning to clear her head and deciding she could do it although finding her legs were shaky.

The sun shone on the garage which was gradually disappearing in all the rough growth which was their garden. Funny how triumphant those thistles looked. She made her unsteady way down the defeated irregular stone path and peered through the broken window. The car was still there of course but Frank, he was also there. He was slumped, breathing deeply in the passenger seat. Beside him in the driving seat an empty vodka bottle. Her mind raced as things fell into line.

"I knew it. I knew it. You've been doing this for ages."

She banged on the side wall and gradually he woke as another piece of glass fell to the ground.

Eventually he came out of the garage and they stood looking at each other strangely without malice, and then together they moved back into the house.

*

Down at the school it was long past going home time. Sonya and Lisette waited in the playground expecting at any moment to spot the dark blue anorak of their father, but today it didn't appear. Their friends had disappeared gradually into the care of parents, grandparents, chirpy childminders and reprimanding nannies. Lisette's class teacher eventually asked them to return inside. Holding hands they were ushered into the Head's office, where they sat in silence. The Head was busy elsewhere in the building, and they looked around the room at the posters on the wall and the piles of new stationery in the corner. Entranced but wary.

Mrs Bridges seemed in a hurry when she did appear. Although she kept smiling she appeared cross with them both.

"The staff have been trying to phone your parents but without success."

She picked up the phone and dialled again.

"No one is answering the phone. That's the fourth time we've tried. I shall have to contact the social services people."

"Who are those people? Social people?" Sonya was genuinely curious but not at all happy with this delay. Sitting here was beginning to feel a bit like the dentist's waiting room.

"They arrange for someone to look after children until their parents can collect them."

Sonya took Lisette's hand. Both sets of eyes grew wide. Sonya turned to reassure her sister. "Don't worry, Ettie, Daddy will be in the garage."

Turning back to the Head she explained. "Daddy is fixing our car. He stays in the garage for ages and ages."

"What about your mother?"

The Head felt it unreasonable that she should have to deal with this, when she had so much other work. It was time for social services to take over.

"She's not well."

"Hmm... so they tell me." The Head was muttering to herself.

"Daddy is fixing the car..."

Lisette found the idea comforting. Then she heard her mother's voice calling outside Mrs Bridge's door. Mum was here. All was okay.

*

Arriving home with the children Eleni noticed Frank had gone up to their bedroom. She settled into the routine of homework, television, food. The shock she suffered on seeing Frank and what was obviously a regular pattern of alcohol in the garage had momentarily cleared her head. She felt strangely energised. Children first blocking out everything else.

Next morning she took the children to school and returned to face Frank. He was waiting, grim-faced as he spoke.

"Why the fucking hell did you start on the sherry?" His tone was one of despair not anger.

She could see it now, as she looked at him. The genuine nature of those early hours spent repairing the car and gradually the onset of alcohol. Funny how she'd stopped visiting him in the garage in the late evenings, and yet an unease had gradually overtaken her. As if she'd known, but she hadn't. Now it seemed obvious. The sheer regularity of shutting himself away down there after the kids were in bed and sometimes not joining her in bed until she was sleeping.

"Everything started to feel wrong, Frank. I sort of knew things were going all wrong. I'd never drunk sherry before. Funny stuff. At first felt more like a children's party drink."

"Yeah. True, true. You used to drink 'very, very dry white wine', and never more than a tipple."

He was slumped on the settee with a mug of very strong coffee. He felt as if he was peering at her and she was a distance away. He had, he knew, become addicted long before she started on the sherry.

"Remember the social worker is coming at eleven thirty this morning."

"Who?"

"The woman… about the children."

He swallowed three aspirins and started to wonder if he should go out and leave Eleni to deal with it. The garage loomed in his mind. His place of solace, not really any more…

*

When the social worker came, Eleni went to the kitchen to make tea and took a few swigs of sherry from the bottle. In her mind she knew she must go to the shops soon. More cooking needed to be done. Last of the kids' prepared meals was waiting in the fridge. Frank had at least managed to put the home-made soup simmering on the hotplate. She struggled with tiredness but a sense of being in a crisis drove her on.

The social worker started talking about the positive aspects of their parenting 'of which there were many' but then switched to the late pick-up at the school yesterday. "Mrs Brooks reported that you were so unsteady on your feet that two staff members and then your children had to help you keep a balance. School staff watched you leave by the school gate."

Eleni didn't argue because she knew it was true.

When the social worker asked where Frank was, Eleni began to tell the full story. The woman went to the garage and indeed Frank was in there now and actually raised his glass to her.

"I'm here about the children."

He didn't respond except to raise his glass again.

Things couldn't get much worse. This was the end. Eleni felt she was holding a glass that had gradually cracked and was now in pieces.

*

The outcome was that the children were fostered for two weeks at a home close by where they could attend the same school, and their mother went into a residential therapy place for one week and agreed to have a second week at home alone, but going in daily to collect the kids from school and take them to their foster carer. Their father, however, agreed to go into rehab for six months. The children were placed on the Child Protection Register.

Eleni returned home after one week as planned and agreed to attend a weekly counselling session, during which she continued to talk about the creeping fears and doubts she had had that something was going wrong and her foolishness at not wanting to 'put the cards on the table' with Frank. Relatively quickly she reverted to her old strengths and never really lost the confidence of the girls.

Within two months she was given translating work by a London borough, and with her confidence back on board she started to laugh scornfully at the sherry bottles when passing by them in the local shop.

*

"But, Dad, when will you be home?"

Their voices lingered in his mind sometimes distant other times in the forefront. It was always the social worker or her assistant who brought Lisette and Sonya to visit him, and they brought their drawings of the sun and flowers in full bloom and spiders dangling confidently on webs and bees working in unison taking pollen to the beehive. He started to pin them up in his small room around his bed.

He was told things were going well at home. His wife was taking on work and his children were still enjoying school and getting good marks for their work. They handled the fostering fortnight well because they had the resources – treated it as an adventure.

When they left he often felt a surge of confidence. He was in trouble, yes, but he was going to learn from them, his kids. He wasn't going down. He'd grown up in rural Devon, now he was in a big, big town. The land had given him something solid and fertile to work on and he could work on those things wherever he lived. Come winter, come spring...

But later things often swung the other way. Like today, after a heartening visit and time spent with his daughters his surge of optimism suddenly slumped. Here he was in the evening discussion group listening to himself describing his desire for vodka to a glum audience, his love of inebriation, the sheer wonder and quiet excitement he experienced in his garage. The solicitor opposite looked at him solemnly and said nothing but then he hardly responded to anything that was said. He sat silently listening as if he was in a court room. The returned soldier burst out, "No mate. Don't. Don't," and then repeated himself, his tone rising to hysterical levels.

Frank looked round the group.

"No mate. Don't. Don't."

Two staff members led the demobbed man away from the group as his cries of 'Don't. Don't' took him back to the slaughter he had been forced to commit in a lonely spot beside a rock in some barren country.

"Shit. He's in a bad way." The engine driver put his head in his hands. The group co-ordinator looked at the solicitor who remained mute. Frank withdrew into himself, thinking this was all so unnecessary. He needn't be here. He was like his daughters, he had what they had... these 'resources' the social worker had mentioned. He shouldn't be here.

The engine driver was talking on about his whisky flask which had belonged to his grandfather. The swigs had been automatic, part of a sort of family pattern. A continuation.

There was a general empathetic nodding around the group. In the quiet that followed they heard the recently demobbed soldier upstairs screaming "Don't. Don't."

*

It seemed a long time to Frank before he had completed five months in rehab. His moods were now more stable and he'd talked about employment with a visiting officer who had raised possibilities.

"You grew up on the land and have a diploma in agriculture. Eventually you could be employed by a supermarket. There's work sorting out contracts with farmers, you know, size of carrots and all that…"

"Really."

Frank frowned and then it started to make sense.

"You mean contracts between…"

"Yes. Farmers and supermarkets. A big thing these days. You'd have to learn all the basic supermarket tasks first. Also after leaving here you must return to the Post Office work for at least six months and prove you can keep off the dreaded alcohol."

"Yeah… I see…"

He looked at the employment officer who seemed to wear his suit with a certain discomfort. Frank could see him, on arriving home, climbing into his joggers before the outside door closed. He smiled and wanted to be away from here, from all this talk, talk, talk about alcohol, he wanted to mix and chat with normal folks.

"Do you drink?"

The man grinned.

"Eh. Yes. I do. I love the stuff. Well, will you think about all I've said?"

"Certainly."

Not long after he was surprised to be visited by the social worker and Eleni. It seemed Eleni hovered behind the social worker. Was she just observing, Frank thought? The social worker talked of all the positive things in their care of the girls, just like she did in that first interview. Then she asked if Frank had any particular questions to ask. He looked at his wife.

"So they're okay are they?"

"Er... yes... Except they constantly ask when you will be home. Fret a bit late at night."

His heart leapt. Just to hear her voice. He felt like a tired working horse after a hard day in the fields stepping, nearly stumbling, into the stable.

"Ah... I see."

"We thought you should know that." The social worker broke into a long silence.

His heart seemed to settle to a strong steady beat.

"They're doing well... there was a child protection conference last week and your wife attended, as well as the school."

Eleni added, "And Sonya is taking the extra music lessons on offer."

He wanted to ask more but couldn't seem to form the words. He was looking at Eleni's shoes and calves. Dark tights with no ladders. He put his head down overcome by a kind of grief.

"Please leave me. Let me think."

They left and he didn't look up until the door closed. Then he went to the window and watched them getting into the social worker's car. Ironically he saw it was a green Mondeo, C registration. Eleni turned and looked at the building before getting into the car. That same look. Sort of wistful and calm. Their relationship just might be surviving. Frank turned away and went to the exercise room, still muddled in his head but feeling solemnly positive that he could exist without that dreaded vodka.

'They survived being fostered because they have the resources.'

He stretched flat out on the floor lifting both legs slowly.

*

For the first time just Eleni turned up next day with Lisette and Sonya. They all talked at the same time until Eleni quietened the girls down and told how they had had Michelle to do an overnight visit earlier this week. Lisette did little dance steps around his chair.

"Lovely little girl," Eleni said, "And I had a coffee with her mother when I took her home."

"And you went to the council protection... thing... meeting."

"Oh. The conference. Yes. I did... It was... it was okay. No more legal action planned in our case at the moment."

Eleni looked at him and held his eyes. Then she smiled, still holding his gaze.

"Ah... and I can come home then." He couldn't believe that he was saying this.

"Certainly can... we need a father in the home."

When they left he felt a surge of confidence. His kids. His wife. He would look further into that marketing job. Meanwhile back to being a postman.

They'd save for that visit to Budapest. By air of course. What the hell had made him think they would drive. It had grown from nothing that idea and then he'd milked it in a self-indulgent way. They had been in trouble no doubt about that but he was on his way out of it. Heading upwards. He would get rid of the Ford and buy four bicycles. Eleni always talked of cycling in her childhood and youth, and where they lived it was a good area for bikes, many off-road cycle tracks, and that garage, so dilapidated. He would knock it down and build a greenhouse.

He'd needed that eye-to-eye thing with Eleni just now. It was the look that in the past they had often given to each other before going up to bed. They both understood what that meant. She'd also talked of more translation work with Southwark Council.

Smiling inside to himself he felt the confidence of a steady man of the land making a future in the London suburbs, and yes he might even have to have that vasectomy.

Snack Lunch: Saturday

Mum, do you know we have four times as many teenage single mothers as they have in France.

Really. But why are you bringing this up now?

It's in my French text book.

Emily! Are you sure?

Yes, Mum.

Well you've got to think about this Emily. We've talked about this before. Some young people… they don't take time… you don't have to rush into sex.

I know that. You've got to wait for each other, haven't you? I mean to have simultaneous orgasm.

Emily. I don't mean that. I mean, being a virgin. It's okay. There's no hurry.

Whatever.

Not 'whatever' Emily. Never 'whatever' when it comes to sex and your own fertility.

Don't worry, Mum. I've just done a pregnancy test and I'm not pregnant.

Come Fly With Me

The doctor approached the flat with a speedy business-like gait, but walking this fast never stopped him engaging with a building. He was young and London intrigued him. The metal stairs were on the outside of the building and as he ascended he observed the discoloured once-red bricks and a lift shaft that looked like a scarred, disused chimney. One of the flats had caught fire some months ago and was scorched, windows boarded up. The stairs were slippery and treacherous in winter. The smell on the corridors and around the lift was of bodily substances excreted in moments of acute need, or at other times angrily, rebelliously, guiltily. An uncomfortable reminder of how we aren't always in control. Bodily things take over. What we all hope never happens does happen.

As he approached No.21 the wind scurried around the floor on the outside corridor on level two. He observed a Kentucky Fried Chicken carton only partially consumed, and then a pile of dog shit. Not unfamiliar. Step carefully. Don't sniff. Approaching in a balloon-like manner was a supermarket bag, swerving, bumping, circling and then resting. Ahead he could see the Thames, grey-brown tinged with purple and, in the distance, stood the Millennium Dome. Firm, squat, glinting in the half light. A friendly alien.

A young woman in a trench coat opened the door to him and said she was Rachael Richards, the social worker. Their quick shared smile held a hint of conspiracy. Inside the old lady was on the settee, seeming to be enjoying the attention. She already had two visitors, now another.

"Here he is, Ethel. He's here now. This is the doctor we told you about."

The social worker smiled and gestured to the doctor who reached out to shake Ethel's hand.

"Don't get up, Ethel."

Settling himself beside her on the settee he opened his briefcase. There was a pause and Ethel looked at the social worker, who seemed so pleased to have them all together like this, and then there was Liz who looked sort of relieved as if a weight was being lifted from her shoulders. Ethel liked Liz. Liz, her mate, her friend person, who came every day and did things. She couldn't remember when Liz started these visits. It seemed like a long time ago. The doctor spoke English well but the old lady knew he was foreign. He wasn't black, dark brown or any of the varying degrees of olive, but she was a Londoner and she knew sounds. Like the way he said her name, making the 't' just a bit too hard.

"I'm going to give you three words, Ethel, and then I shall ask you to tell me what they are. I want you to remember them."

"Book. First word... book."

He was trying to get eye contact, but Ethel was avoiding it, not wanting to be too co-operative. Why should she be? She preferred to look at Liz's hand which kept reaching out to touch her shoulder reassuringly. Liz was her home help who had appeared one day, just walked in like a friendly busybody, and together they had started to clear up all the piles of clothes and newspapers, soiled laundry and used tissues. It was something to do with the council. There'd been pigeon droppings thick on the balcony. Liz had chopped away at all that, cleared it off, and all that frozen food which had been left standing on the kitchen table for months had been thrown away. Bit of a waste, but Liz had insisted. Now and then they had found a photograph or a letter, or piece of jewellery which they had saved. Not that she ever knew where they were saved. Saved somewhere but lost again. For Ethel that was how everything felt.

"Plate. That's the second word, Ethel. As I explained. I am giving you three words and then I shall ask you to tell me what they are... remember them."

"What?"

Ethel looked bewildered but noted he was a nice young man very intent on his task.

"Did you hear the word I just said? Plate. Plate. And before that I said Book."

"I can't hear him. Tell him, Liz."

Well she could hear him but she didn't know what on earth he was going on about. The social worker was wearing her trench coat. She almost always wore it. Ethel liked the coat. It reminded her of something she couldn't, just couldn't recall properly.

"Plate."

Ethel wondered vaguely why the young man kept saying words, but her attention was on trench coat, who had something to do with Liz. These two seemed to get on fine, and sometimes Liz would say she would have to let the council know, and that meant trench coat. She never minded. She trusted them both. Just now they were explaining to the young man that she was not deaf.

"Only a slight hearing impairment," said trench coat. Ethel stopped paying attention to the words and looked approvingly at the expensive quality material of the doctor's jacket.

"Can you repeat that for me, Ethel?"

Ethel frowned, it was worse than being physically examined by a doctor or a dentist even. For some reason she was reminded of her old friend Ruby. Ruby would laugh. She wouldn't have any cop with either. Con men the lot of them is what Ruby said. That was after Ruby had gone into hospital with an awful pain in her stomach and they'd taken out her appendix, but the pain had persisted and turned out to be a tumour.

The room was silent. Ethel noted trench coat smilingly accepted a mug of tea from Liz, and Ethel started to smile herself but no one would have known. For years now her false teeth dropped when she tensed and lifted the corners of her mouth and she had to tighten her lips to keep the teeth in. She was not aware that her smiles did not show, and sometimes she felt angry with people for being so mean spirited and not responding to her smiles. She couldn't stop thinking of her friend now. Ruby had never forgiven them. Always regretted losing her appendix. 'Just in case…' that is what the doctor at the hospital had said to her. 'Just in case.' As if it was alright to take something out, 'just in case.' Of course, when you're lying flat on a hospital bed you don't argue with doctors. 'I want it back,' Ruby had kept saying. 'It's a piece of me and there was nothing wrong with it.'

"Ethel. Are you concentrating? The third word is Knife."

"Knife." Ethel spoke and he nodded, pleased that this time she seemed to be responding. She was aware they were talking about her, something about her living here since the block went up in the early sixties. Husband? Yes. Trench coat said she'd had one, and hearing this Ethel had a fleeting glimpse of the soft fine fair skin on his face which had become softer and sweeter as he grew older.

'And her good friend Ruby always lived next door… died of cancer 2 years ago… they were widowed about the same time.'

Ethel's thoughts of Ruby hovered. Ruby's touch. Nothing felt like Ruby's hands on her head, parting the strands of hair and firmly winding and weaving them into a plait.

The young man sipped from his mug.

"I want you to repeat the three words I gave you, Ethel."

What was he talking about? Three words? And they were all looking, waiting. She didn't have to answer questions in her own home. Didn't they realise she was free now, that she had nothing she had to do anymore, she needn't remember anything. She could put what she liked in and out of the freezer because Liz always came in and sorted it out and heated her meal every day in that little oblong thing that worked like magic. Now what was it called?

"Three words? The first? Ethel, tell me the first of the three words I gave you."

The room had gone quiet. Three pairs of eyes were on her.

"Microwave."

Ethel just wanted to shut him up and clear the air. She was becoming uncomfortable with all the suspense in the atmosphere, but she understood now he wanted her to say three words.

"Thank you, Ethel. And the second word?"

"Appendix."

They all looked down as if they were sorry about Ruby's appendix.

"Yes, and number three?"

"Yorkshire pudding."

She thought that would amuse them. It was beginning to seem like a Christmas party game.

"Whatever is that, Ethel?"

The young man smiled at her and Ethel hesitated, relieved when trench coat answered for her. She heard 'flour and egg', 'traditional', and 'rises'. She remembered how her husband had... funny she couldn't quite recall his name... had loved Yorkshire Pudding. Liz jumped up and prepared to leave. Apparently she had to visit two other people this morning. Ethel was then aware that the doctor was shaking her hand, his papers replaced in his briefcase. She felt a burst of optimism. They had all been good company, all these young people. She expected them all to go. Out of the door. Now you see them, now you don't. Gone in a flash, leaving her to herself, but she began to see that trench coat was staying on.

"Would you like more tea, Ethel?

Now what was this about? Ethel wanted only to be left alone now to think about her husband, dwell on the memory of that soft, fine skin. She said she would like more tea, so trench coat disappeared into the kitchen and reappeared with another mug.

"There's something serious I want to talk to you about…"

Try as she could Ethel could not now dissociate herself from the peachy texture of her husband's cheeks.

"We've had neighbours phoning in saying that you were out in your nightie at four o'clock this morning. Do you remember being out?"

Ethel began to feel some of trench coat's seriousness and unease.

"No. No. I don't know…"

The words drifted vaguely into thoughts. All the smiling had stopped. She felt anxious now and didn't know why.

"You were knocking on doors in the block, asking if they could direct you to the Post Office."

"Who was… doing that? Was it… was it me? No."

"Yes. It was you and your handbag was all unzipped and full of notes. The neighbour at number twelve eventually brought you back to your flat. She phoned my office two days ago. It's not the first call we've had like this about you waking people in the night."

"My bills… I was going to pay my bills…"

"You can't go out in the night like that. You put yourself at risk and anyway it was too cold to be in just a nightie… and, another thing, no one likes having their door bell rung at four in the morning."

There was a long pause. The atmosphere had made her withdraw further into herself. She was going over some good things. The way he'd stayed faithful. Such a handsome man. Just the two of them all those years. No babies.

"Paying bills isn't a problem for you, Ethel. You've allowed Liz to do those things for you."

Liz. Oh yes Liz. Ethel responded positively and then noted that trench coat was saying goodbye, she would be back and reminding her to think seriously about these outings in the night. Ethel felt upset now. There was just a glimmer in her mind, a kind of recognition and acknowledgement that there was some substance in what trench coat was saying.

Left to her own devices she went out onto her little balcony to feed the pigeons. They came in a rush as soon as they heard her opening the door. They flustered and pushed, chuckled and gobbled. Years and years ago her mother had made pigeon pie, and as they all sat at the table her father would always say, 'not much breast on these birds.' He made it sound like the worst of all crimes 'not much breast,' and the statement always made her and her brother helpless with repressed laughter. Silly birds. She stared at the scene on her balcony. Their greediness suddenly irritated her. They were so overweight. Some of them took ages to lift themselves into flight, and then they wobbled badly as they rose above her balcony. They were amazingly resistant to being shooed if there was still food around. She felt a familiar surge of impatience. So bumptious. So fat. Stupid things. Their take-off was now so slow, anyone could grab them.

Down below there was the sound of teenagers in the street. Schools closed, darkness coming on early. The atmosphere down there was taut. A traffic jam on the south circular caused the odd vehicle to speed crazily along the side street passing her balcony. Nothing seemed to matter out there except getting where they were going. These times people would pass by anything without stopping so long as they could get home, lights on, familiar smells, warmth, television, pieces of well-known furniture, the little conglomerate that was their nest.

Ethel closed the balcony door. The lights were on outside but it was her way not to switch her own lights on straight away. She liked to look out of her window, all seeing but not seen. Canary Wharf was flashing and the illuminated Dome looked as if it had just landed, and was soon to take off into outer space, full of lucky and important people. Or it might not. It might be an extraordinary shellfish which would soon make its way back to the North Sea. To Ethel it was like fairyland out there, and that was a good thing. She couldn't tell which building was which but she liked the sparkle. Ruby had pointed out the Dome some years ago when it was being built but Ethel had long forgotten all the details. Its significance was not as important as its familiarity.

Bedtime soon, but what was it Liz kept saying. Don't go to bed too early and don't go to bed in your clothes. 'Twirly... twirly, Ethel. No wonder you're up at four in the morning.' She smiled to herself and felt better now. All that was fuss about nothing, but in many ways she liked the fuss. They all crowded in on her sometimes. Ethel this, Ethel that... and they were agitated, worried. Smiling and worried. She was a funny mixture of things when they came in here with their notebooks. Cross. Thankful. Amused. Proud. Fear and giggles all beaten together and ready for the oven.

It all happened again three weeks later, and this time the assembled group included a man with a beard and a clipboard. Ethel listened but didn't really know what it was all about. Her mind would not hold on to the words. The sounds were familiar but the meanings flitted across her mind like loose leaves on her balcony. Wouldn't stay, wouldn't hold.

The social worker was speaking and looking grimmer by the minute. The last call she had taken from a resident in this block had been uncompromising, 'Get that old Doris out of 'ere or next thing'll be she'll be found in the river.' Then she had read the reports from Liz about the pigeons. The bearded man was introduced to Ethel, and her mind fleetingly registered 'health and environ-something'. She thought he was nice with her interests at heart. They kept coming, these council people. She expected she deserved it. Liz was speaking.

"I found them in the spare room when I opened the door yesterday. Since we've cleared up in there I don't go in often, but Ethel had lost her purse and…"

The other two were looking at Liz who was now describing the pigeons.

"…there were these two birds, nearly dead, just fluttering a bit… but, worse of all, when I went to put her meal in the microwave I found this… er… dead bird."

Liz shuddered and turned to Ethel.

"You remember, don't you? When I opened the door… the microwave, the dead bird?"

As she spoke, Liz put her hand apologetically on Ethel's shoulder.

"It had been sort of cooked… in… er… its feathers and you said to me… well it deserved it."

Ethel was aware of a sudden silence, and the environmental health officer, accustomed as he was to all kinds of practices related to animals and birds, found himself struggling with an urge to vomit and he couldn't help wondering about the exact state of the bird when it was placed in the microwave. As he spoke, his eyebrows were raised as he looked at the social worker.

"So… what was the state of the bird when… the pigeon… was it alive when Ethel put it in the microwave?"

Ethel looked at Liz, who gave a quick weak smile, and wondered why they were all going on about pigeons. Nothing but a nuisance those birds. If she had her time again she would not have started feeding them.

"Ethel. How did the birds get in your flat in the first place?"

Liz's question. They all seemed to be waiting. Ethel looked at the lapels on trench coat. How level, how balanced. Her husband had been fond of his jackets. The bearded man and trench coat were now standing on her balcony and Liz was beside her flicking through some papers, holding a pale pink biro in one hand. Ethel found herself thinking of Ruby's appendix and then, at the same time, of her husband. Images of flesh changing from flaccid to rigid made her chuckle. It was all so silly now. People's bits and pieces. Trench coat was still grim.

"Ethel, you must realise. You can't live like this. You really must consider moving. Somewhere where you'll be looked after, kept safe."

Ethel looked at trench coat's teeth. A reasonable set. She felt she knew them well. The environmental health officer heard pigeons chortling outside. He was pleased he was not a social worker. Liz rushed in enthusiastically.

"All your meals prepared, plenty of company all day."

"And…" Trench coat looked at Liz and then at Ethel as she spoke.

"Your own small room. You could take a few of your own things from here, like your nice tea service and the wedding photographs."

Ethel was continuing to peer at trench coat's face. She noted that it was not quite so grim now. Whatever it was she was trying to bring about was most likely for the best. Okay, she was going. She would go. She would soon be out of here, flying along the river passing Canary Wharf, Tower Bridge and Big Ben. The bearded man was collecting his papers. From what he knew of the way his council worked this woman would soon be in a residential home, and as far as he was concerned it was about time too. He said his goodbyes, seeming to bow slightly to Ethel on the settee, and let himself out onto the outside corridor. As he descended the metal stairs he cast a sympathetic eye on the pigeons.

Breakfast: Saturday

Tim, have you finished your porridge?

Yep. I'm thinking.

Your lesson's at 10.00.

Mum, why do old folks, you know, they get all droopy and wrinkly and can't walk properly...

Yes. Most of us will if we live...

But then they say they need help.

Of course.

Sometimes they say it and that man on television wants us all to do our bit or something.

Yes.

What if there's nobody there to do their bit?

That's when the public services, the council get involved.

Why can't we just leave them in their houses, then we could...

Tim. You're being silly. Then they would suffer a lot.

No... I'm just thinking. Why don't we leave them indoors, nobody would know until they came to clean windows or for charity money. Just leave them there with their dogs and cats.

What are you talking about? That would be inhumane... and an awful mess. Would you want that to happen to you?

Well the council could collect them in those big lorries.

You mean the rubbish collection.

Otherwise it would start to smell awful. Don't worry, I'm off now, Mum, to my flute lesson.

Dirty Water

At the top of the hill there was a water tower, red brick with a pointed slate roof. It provided clean water for the area. Almost as important to some, it served as a landmark that could be seen from the M25 and further north on the M11. Houses of Victorian, Edwardian and modern designs clustered on the summit. There were pubs galore, one on top of the hill, and others on either side of the descending slopes and round corners at all ends. Across the road was woodland which had been there for centuries, now incorporating an underground reservoir covered with lush green grass, and back in the woods at the west end a building erected to commemorate the conquest of the Malabar Coast by the British in 1755. Was it a castle or a tower? Uncertainty reigned. No one was quite sure, and now it was dilapidated but defiantly tall.

Bernard steered his wheelchair out of the pub and made his way along the pavement. Only a short distance to his home, going downhill but he had good brakes. He was wearing corduroy trousers, and the stump of his right leg wobbled slightly as he crossed the threshold into his living room. The television screen was large and dominated the room and in one corner was a toy train set, laid out on a table. On the other side shelves held piles of magazines and rows of neatly stacked videos and DVDs. It was a knock-through lounge-diner, now converted into a bed-sit to accommodate his disabilities.

Since his stroke and the amputation of his gangrenous leg, he was confined to his chair. Crazy really because all those years in the army he'd never had an injury. He'd moved to this converted ground floor flat after discharge from hospital and had been set up with what the council then called a Care Package, which was all these women coming in and out preparing his food and all the other stuff they did. At the time he hadn't expected it to be much help at all, but it was alright. It worked okay. They came in pairs and they were all young. That was after the older woman came to see what was needed and set it all up. Yes, he knew them all and their ways, the giggly ones, the ones who touched him reassuringly, the ones who had beautiful bosoms, the ones who were always late. He laughed to himself. They were okay.

In the early days he had complained in the pub about all the compulsory forms which went with the service.

"They keep changing the names and type of forms, asking me to sign and re-sign. The times I've done it and redone it, you'd think I was agreeing to sell myself to the devil... Have a drink yourself, Terry."

"What I wonder is what these places do with all the waste paper," laughed Terry from behind the bar.

"Probably blocking toilets in Australia." Ernie proffered, standing beside Bernard at the bar looking at his neat collar and tie and thinking that for a cripple this man was always so spruce. Likely a product of his army days.

"How do you arrive at that, Ernie?" asked Terry, still smiling as he pulled another pint.

"It's obvious ain't it... they're upside down ain't they."

Bernard thought Ernie was in the pub far too much for a working man. They all took a thoughtful sip.

"Can't you just ignore... um?" Ernie again. "Put um down the loo."

"No. If I did it would all stop... these women would stop coming."

Bernard laughed. "Gradually perhaps, but... like grind to a halt. The jolly council have your bollocks really, when it comes to."

Well that was over a year ago and all the paperwork and form-filling which came with these women certainly was a nuisance, but the letter which came this morning was downright disturbing. He had gone to the pub with it in his pocket, and with Ernie's ever-sympathetic gaze had been tempted to talk. He'd started out at the bar.

"This morning there's this letter. They're threatening to stop the visits, they call it 'terminate the community' something or other…"

Something warned him then to be careful. It wasn't really a matter to blab about.

"They can't do that, mate."

Ernie was staring at Bernard's trousers. He couldn't believe a man could survive with bits like that missing, and those cord trousers were a touch 'well-to-do'.

"Is it the NHS?"

"No Ernie, it's the council."

"What's Council Tax for then?"

"The council authorised… you know… set it up, and I contribute."

"Sounds a right mess. What's the letter then, mate?"

"Oh this and that." Bernard hesitated and reminded himself to keep his mouth shut. Ernie waited, staring down as he often did at the man in the wheelchair. The poor chap had what he'd always dreaded, the loss of a limb. He came and went okay though. Sometimes he looked tired and turned the wheels with effort, needing to pause at intervals, and at such times his hands shook so that he took ages to light his cigar. Often lit it just before leaving the bar and the landlord never commented. Always drank shorts, never beer. Never went for a leak.

"Well what?"

Bernard didn't regard Ernie as his equal when it came to personal matters like this one, and he must be careful, but he was a bit desperate to have someone to talk to.

"Well it's all these young women that come in and out."

"You're not bonking them are you, Bernard?"

He allowed Ernie to have his cackle. Then he decided that was enough. That really was enough. He wasn't going to expand further. Not today. Not any day with such like as Ernie around.

"Another drink, mate?" Ernie was looking at him quizzically.

This time the Landlord served them, commenting in his quiet way. "Having a bit of trouble with your holiday package are you, Bernard?"

Everybody grinned at the bar, except Bernard, even the man who hadn't heard all the conversation and was at the bar to take drinks back to a table.

"Nothing serious." Bernard was trying to tone things down. Instinctively he now felt cautious about saying any more. He began the process of lighting a cigar and added, "Just Council mumbo jumbo… and it's not Care Package any more, it's a Community Care Schedule."

They all chuckled and Bernard struck another match.

*

Nena and her partner turned up to heat his lunch. She was one of the regulars and today she had a new girl with her, introducing her as having an induction week to find out how to do things. Bernard thought she looked to be barely eighteen and she was shaking a bit as they seated him on the commode. It took two to do Bernard's transfers. She smelt like the whiskey soup his grandmother used to make. It was supposedly parsnip with a dash of whisky but it made his grandfather's face swell up like a balloon.

Nena was from Somalia and her skin was the purest black with not a blemish, her cheekbones were high and her rear protruded gracefully from her slim erect body.

Bernard watched thinking he had never before seen such a shapely backside. Lately he'd been waking in the night with Nena's rear end fixed like a picture in his mind. Those shapely buttocks. He knew by heart every kind of dress – the jeans, brown culottes, skirt, and she always addressed him with full eye contact, giving him all her concentration. She cared. In his dreams Nena walked in an area lush and green, carrying on her head a shapely urn, and he watched, obscured by an abundance of ferns, sweating, aroused, straining. Calling out. Then running towards her on two legs just as she disappeared.

Today she took his hot meal from the microwave and put it down on his little table which was virtually covered with cassettes and cigar ash. The other girl was emptying the ashtrays and putting the cassettes back on the rack. Nena sniffed the familiar smell of stale ash and wondered why the authorities didn't stop him smoking. He was often coughing. With his disabilities he couldn't afford to damage his lungs. She bent to pick up a video case from the floor. Then Bernard asked her to sweep ash from the carpet. She went quickly for the hand brush and shovel. He watched her movements as she now crouched with her knees spread wide, industriously sweeping. A few more minutes and it was her 'goodbye smile', and 'see you tomorrow, Bernard.'

The smell of the new girl lurked in his senses for some time but he managed eventually to nod off, only to be awakened by a car alarm going off in the street outside. He picked up the newspaper and checked the racing on television. Then he looked at his handwritten notes where he had his carers all listed in secret code. It was a complicated timetable but he'd cracked it. This one was 'G'. They all had their attributes. He reached for his remote and switched on his DVD.

Amergit heard the music in the background when she spoke to Bernard on his entry phone. She was arriving for his teatime visit, usually a sandwich, hot drink and a help to the toilet. When she entered the room he was taken aback to see, instead of her usual very young partner, an older woman. Looked to be in her fifties, at least.

Hearing the music filled Amergit with dread. Surely, not again! Those films. The semi-dark room, the pulsing beat of the background music, the bodies on the screen. Why did this nice man do it? She had no words in relation to all this only a sensation of shame and discomfort. The way the women were so overpowered, so sexual, so vulnerable. It was the forcing that distressed her, the brutality of the men, the way they thrust themselves on the women, penetrating them like, well… like animals she had once watched as a child. Something about the bodies confused her, so naked, so unlike real live people and yet so like what you always knew was there, was possible. It gave her a funny feeling. Sometimes she stared, transfixed.

His fingers went so quick to his remote and the screen went blank. Mavis introduced herself and said, "You needn't put the telly off, Bernard."

"Oh, I must. We like to talk, don't we 'git?"

Of course, he would have left it on as usual but with this new woman. No way. He knew what being checked was… he'd been in the army hadn't he… her eyes were all over the place. This woman was to do with the letter this morning.

Amergit accepted his mispronunciation of the 'g' in her name. Lots of English people did it. Mavis went to the kitchen. Amergit looked at Bernard and noticed he was staring at her chest. Then he closed his eyes.

"Are you tired, Bernard?" She wanted so much to be of help to someone so unfortunate, so disadvantaged, who needed her. Her mothering-side, which as yet had not had any real practice, was somehow, at the moment, more developed in her than, say, in her sisters, who could be quite callous in their attitude. She might one day train to be a nurse. It was such a pity with this man, in a wheelchair after such an active life in the army. Certainly hadn't lost it like some of the people she went in to. But…

Through the window she could see the water tower. Today the workmen were busy there, up and down ladders. They said there were problems – something to do with the water pressure. She liked it here on the hill. Her mother seemed pleased when she said she was working here, away from the high rises and inoperative lifts, looking after what her mother called "the nicer people." Her father had been a doctor in Delhi and, when he died prematurely, her mother had brought her small daughters to England to live with her relatives. Big sister Albinda had married into the family of a local Estate Agent and her mother often said to Amergit that her father would not have considered this a good marriage. This made no sense to Amergit. Her brother-in-law worked hard in his father's business and provided well for her sister and also his mother-in-law who was always putting him down. Amergit disliked the idea of privilege based on birth and her education at the local school she had attended just up the road had reinforced this dislike. All too often though she observed that privilege worked the same here as it seemed to in India.

She turned to help Mavis lift Bernard onto his commode. This man's shoulders reminded her of her father, when as a child she would stand behind his chair and put her arms around his neck. She had loved her father who used to nurse her and read to her from English books. Were he alive now he would want her to do more study, get more skills. When he died she had cried miserably through many nights, longing for him to kneel beside her bed and smooth the hair from her hot forehead.

As she bent over Bernard his face rested against her breast and she felt his nose sink into the soft flesh. It was uncomfortable. She went quickly over, in her head, how she had been trained to lift so that this did not happen. He was breathing heavily as if concentrating too much. She seemed to be doing everything right. Perhaps it was Bernard, through no fault of his own, losing his balance. Mavis stopped and insisted they put Bernard back in his chair and redo the movement.

"Let's get it right this time." Mavis spoke looking straight into his eyes and her voice was a touch reprimanding.

He groaned but his nose was nowhere near her breast on this second go.

As soon as the door closed behind them and with the scent and feel of Amergit's bosom fresh in his senses Bernard reached for the remote. He was at the place where the woman on screen suddenly relaxed and opened her legs. Under pressure, of course, but that was the way he liked it. This was one of his favourites. He shuffled into a comfortable position and prepared to see it all over again.

When the film finished it was gone six o'clock. Outside the traffic had gathered momentum, becoming the usual snarling, revving, familiar mass. Tonight there was a crashing sound followed by car doors slamming and voices raised. He replayed some of the film. Then it was approaching bedtime.

Now, who would be in next? The carer coming in later for the 'put to bed' would be Kelly and her accomplice, the one who giggled all the time. Bernard smiled to himself and thought of Kelly's solid hips in her tight jeans, and the way her accomplice was so placid and sort of mesmerised when he left his film on. The pair of them would carry on preparing him for bed, grinning at each other a bit to save face but looking, oh so alarmed.

The thing was, the big thing here was that they knew, or Kelly knew, that they owed him something. Twice they had not turned up which was serious stuff, enough to get them sacked if it was reported. Each time he had spent the whole night in his wheelchair. He had not reported them and, from the time Kelly had given her excuses and apologies, she had known that in some respects he now had the upper hand. He had said: "I'll keep it in mind, but if it happens again…"

It came naturally to him to use situations like this, a continuation from his army days. He'd put up with their lack of duty so they'd put up with his.

Oh yes. He planned to replay the film he had just watched where the woman was at first reluctant but then became enthusiastic. You could say, hot for it. Very, very hot. Calling out to the man. Reaching out to touch his genitals, seeming to crave with all her body to be touched.

Explored. The girls would watch bits, raise their eyebrows at each other and then glance back at the screen. It meant they took longer and would probably be late for their next put-to-bed.

His entry phone buzzer went just as he started the film again.

"Hello Bernard."

Not Kelly. He frowned. A male voice. "I'm Dennis. Come to do your 'put to bed'."

Now what was going on? Dennis. He didn't want a Dennis. He clicked the video off, and when the carer arrived at his door he was unwelcoming.

"I'm not ready for bed yet. Come back later."

"A wee bit early perhaps. Tomorrow I'll make it half an hour later."

Tomorrow? He had that male nurse, firm, friendly sound.

"Well come back later, I said…"

He detested this bonhomie attitude. The man was a complete stranger. How disrupting when he was just getting in the mood for the 'Kelly gang'.

"I'll report you to my social worker. She stressed the time factor on my care plan. Says it is important for my 'dignity and self-esteem'. Going to bed too early can be depressing."

"Sorry Bernard, but it was your social worker who asked me to come. Says a letter has come to you about your videos etcetera."

"My videos are my own business. Certainly not yours."

"You've received the letter?"

"Haven't the council got anything better to do with their time?"

"Bernard, it's basically this…" Dennis was unruffled by the protests. "We know you've been playing porn when…"

"Rubbish. All rubbish."

"I've got eyes, Bernard. Look at this that you have on now?" Dennis took the remote and pressed the button.

"Now Bernard. Really. Oh look at him. Isn't he... isn't he just! See what I mean? Better put it off, Bernard. It's disgusting."

He allowed himself to be put to bed and when Dennis had gone his words came floating back.

'I've taken over all your care, Bernard. Just cheerful old me. I'm specially skilled in lifting, don't need a helper. Oh except for weekends when Alec or Amir will do it. They share the weekend work. Like me they manage on their own.'

Somebody had reported him. Most likely that 'up front' local girl about three weeks ago. Tracy, that was her name. Perhaps that's where he had made an error of judgement, even if she had been an hour late three days in a row and he hadn't reported her. She'd said something like 'if... you don't turn that fucking thing off, I'll...' As soon as she swore he thought 'now she's done it, I've scored.' Then he quickly realised this was not so. She was one of those local girls who knew her rights, and wouldn't be intimidated. There were a lot of them about these days. Not brain boxes but they knew where they stood and soon let you know. How they got like that he wasn't sure. In his day women would not have spoken out in that manner. It was all that... well, doing the correct thing something or other. Political something. It gave the wrong people the upper hand and women the right to do just about anything they wanted. It had all gone too far. They understood these things in the pub.

He swore to himself. He would complain. He had a case. The council couldn't change his carers on a whim. He didn't pay Council Tax for this sort of thing.

*

Next morning he started to tell the men in the pub that he now had Dennis full-time. He described the video as 'a bit hot.'

"Haven't they got a sense of humour, these women?" The landlord turned away as he served a woman with six gin and tonics. Her mates were laughing uproariously over on the corner table.

"You've got your rights. They couldn't 'configrate' them..." Ernie stared at him.

"Confiscate." Bernard wished he hadn't let Ernie in on this conversation. He noted with displeasure that Ernie was well on the way to being drunk. He, Bernard, couldn't allow himself such indulgences. He had to keep his head clear or God knows where he'd be. Some of these working-class chaps had no self-respect.

On returning to his flat he phoned his social worker. She told him he was lucky to get Dennis. There was a shortage of male carers. He knew it was no good arguing with her. Once she'd made her mind up it was a waste of time. No good playing the 'poor cripple' either. He could hear her response 'No Bernard, you are not a poor cripple, you are relatively wealthy. You are physically challenged and in so many ways you're rising admirably to the challenge.'

He had mimicked her in the pub one day and now thought bitterly about the comments. Ernie had said, "'ere's to you, Bernard, and keep rising to the challenge."

But he didn't rise, not properly. He was damaged, he struggled.

Now he really felt deflated. All those women. No more times. Yet he wasn't going to give up. And yes, there was that new middle-aged woman recently moved into the flat next door. A bit over-friendly. She struck him as being a bit more than sixpence short of a shilling. The sort who should still be living with her mother. Not a bad looker though. He would ask her in one afternoon. See what her reaction was like.

Up on the water tower behind the pub men had been at work all day erecting scaffolding. They would be back tomorrow to start work on the inside piping and the outer brickwork. This job had been planned for months but the right materials had not been available. There was also something wrong with the pumping system. If it wasn't put right it would affect the water supply to the whole area.

Breakfast: Sunday

Mum, what's the difference between soft and hard porn?

Really, Emily, you don't half ask difficult things first thing in the morning. Just sit down and get on with your breakfast.

It's to do with a dream I just had.

Okay. They're both to do with watching other people having sex in various ways.

Both?

Well soft is more about looking at people enjoying it – doing it just for pleasure, and the other is more to do with forcing people into things, manipulation, physical, social pressure – all those things.

But I saw a woman in a film who was tied to the bed and she was enjoying it.

Ah well, she wasn't really being forced then.

You mean she liked being tied up.

Yes. Possibly.

Hmmm… I used to think that word 'porn' was like pawn shops where you take something precious and personal and sell it to get money.

Well it's… you want egg this morning?

I watched a rape scene on TV the other day.

Did that upset you?

Urrgh… in a way, but to be honest, it made me feel a bit sort of…

Not sexy I hope.

Yes. A bit… yes… I'll have a poached egg please.

Ah…
Mum, quick! The toast's burning.

Dreams And Drives

The toddler was making marks on a piece of paper with a red felt pen. Her concentration was disturbed by her brother bursting in on her like he often did straight from school, his face large, body ungainly, his movements unpredictable. He smiled down at her with approval, before going to the kitchen and taking a handful of chocolate wafers from the supermarket bag on the worktop.

Their mother sat down on the settee and opened a can of coke, immediately immersing herself in the film which she had been watching before going out to collect Tommy from school. The sound was turned up loud and she didn't hear the doorbell the first time. When she did hear it she grumbled to herself, picked up her nearly finished can of coke and opened the door. It was Mrs Hall from the flat next door.

"Oh hello Kerry. I hope you don't mind me knocking. I saw you go out for Tommy and you didn't take Emma with you…"

There was a pause and Tommy ran to the door and stared at the neighbour.

"I know it's not my business, but do you think you ought to leave her on her own?"

Kerry was only half listening. She could hear the voices on the television. She'd only just got back into the film which had been on 'pause' while she went out for Tommy. There was about to be a row between the heroine and the manageress in her husband's business.

"She's okay. Look at her. Only takes me twenty minutes."

She stood back and with a sweep of her arm invited the neighbour to take a look at Emma who was now sucking the red pen and the whole area of her mouth was blood red. Kerry took a sip of coke, and was about to close the door but Tommy sidled up to the neighbour and put his arms around her legs, his eyes wide, so wide.

"What do you want, Tommy?"

Vera Hall put her hand on his head. His face was pressing against her stomach. She shifted uneasily. Although she had always had an eye on this child she had never encouraged him to have close physical contact like this. On one occasion she had taken him in for 15 minutes when his mother had gone off to the shops and left him playing down below in the block. She considered him a remarkably beautiful boy but his large dark-brown eyes worried her and she wasn't sure why. It wasn't right the way he was holding onto her now.

"Tommy. Come away from Mrs Hall."

When her son didn't respond his mother took hold of his arm and pulled him roughly back into the room. His arms went limp and he turned and slunk away in the direction of his bedroom as if he was being punished for something really bad.

"It's alright, don't be cross with him, he's only being friendly." Vera spoke with a reassuring tone but she was shocked by the mother's rough handling of the child.

"And don't you go into one of your moods. Do you hear?"

Kerry was yelling at her son and Vera began to withdraw. Uncomfortable. She'd caused another upset now with her worrying. The boy had gone to his room. She couldn't do any more, but she disliked the way Kerry spoke to Tommy, and the way he treated the rebuke so seriously. The mother's mood seemed strangely distracted, that smile so weak as she closed the door. Momentarily she forgot why she had knocked on the door in the first place.

Vera let herself back into her own flat thinking of Tommy. In actual fact, although she didn't know him well, she knew a lot about him. Her sister-in-law was a playground supervisor and dinner lady at his school. It struck Vera as strange that his mother had not seemed more indignant about her knocking on the door like that, just now, being, well, some would be quick to say, downright nosey. Most mothers got angry and offended straight away if a neighbour implied even the slightest hint of neglect on their part. Kerry just seemed impatient to get back inside and get on. She continued to think about it all as she prepared the evening meal. It had been some time now since this mother had moved in next door, straight from the hospital after giving birth to Emma. Gradually it had started to worry Vera. A woman all on her own like this and on level three. No way the children could go out into the garden or anything like that… they were so confined.

Len had reassured her. 'Don't worry yourself. There's lots of single mums in this block and they do a splendid job.' This was husband Len, always creating balance, always aware of her concerns, her anxieties. She'd got the right chap there, Vera thought, and she hadn't been wise as a young girl. There were so many different ways, and 'strays', when you were a young woman and looking back she thought her choice of Len had been more by good luck than careful thought and decision making.

In his room, Tommy was looking at his bed, and out of the window, but nothing registered in his mind except an awful gloom, a darkness that stopped him from seeing. He picked up one of his soft cuddly toys, a hippopotamus, and squeezed its head, distorting its familiar shape. Kerry opened another can of coke and resettled back on the settee, irritated by the interruption, and with herself for not pressing 'pause'. She tried to find the spot in the film where she had been when the bell rang. Then she heard Tommy banging around in his room. She tried to ignore it but it made her angry. Inside she began to harbour familiar feelings of annoyance and dislike for him. He was always making her feel miserable. She shouted from the settee.

"Stop that. Do you hear?"

Emma was pushing the tip of the felt pen up her nose.

"Don't Emmie, you'll hurt yourself."

Kerry spoke more to the television screen than to her daughter. In the movie the woman was driving an open-topped car, scarf flying, cleavage proudly displayed, and the man was looking at her. He adored her. The music was rising to a crescendo. Kerry could see he would soon stop the car and they would start kissing. There was another ring on the doorbell and she moved reluctantly away from the screen. Vera again, saying Tommy had broken his bedroom window. She heard it from her place, didn't Kerry hear it? She waited as Kerry took in the information.

"The little sod!"

Now what would happen? Kerry feared he'd get her evicted if he kept behaving this bad. He had already chipped the wood on his bedroom door. Always banging at it with things. She stormed into the bedroom and found Tommy pacing his room, scowling.

"You rotten little pig. Look! Look what you've done."

One large pane of glass was shattered, the bottom half knocked out altogether.

He didn't cry when she started to slap him. He never did which made her all the more furious. He did what he always did, he curled up into a fat ball and it was hard to get at him. Then he started to grunt and snort and Kerry gave up in exasperation.

Vera was playing with Emma in the lounge when Kerry reappeared.

"He's a bit worked up, Kerry, that's all. They get like that after school." She wanted to create calm and resorted to her reassuring tone.

"I remember my Raymond. He did it a couple of times. It's being so good at school, you see... trying so hard to behave themselves... then at home..."

Actually Raymond had cracked not smashed their window. No he'd only done it once but... Kerry was banging around in the kitchen and hardly heard these remarks. She was missing her film. Yet again Tommy had taken away one of her best moments, and now here was this woman again interrupting and carrying on. He was getting way over the top. He was trouble that boy.

"I tell you. I had it. My Raymond did it... and in temper." Vera persisted, wanting so much to smooth things over, bring out some shared concern in Kerry, but this mother wasn't taking any notice.

Kerry still wasn't listening. Her eyes went from the screen to Emma.

"Come here, Emmie. I've got something for you."

Emma left Vera and supported herself along the edge of the settee, once falling backwards onto her bottom, then struggling up and finally plonking herself down beside her mother. She was given a whole packet of sweets, all in wrappers.

"Aren't you a lovely girl. Mummy loves you. Come and give Mummy a kiss."

Vera decided to leave. She couldn't hear a sound from Tommy upstairs. She felt defeated. Naughty to break the window but Kerry did not seem to understand him. She withdrew again, telling herself it wasn't her business and that she had to be careful or she would be called a 'busy body'. The mother obviously resented these intrusions. Perhaps more harm than good. Kerry didn't respond to the "Bye for now," and the click of the latch.

When Tommy eventually came sullenly back into the living area, she put a burger and chips into the microwave.

"I'm going to ring your father and tell him what you've done. How bad and 'orrid you are."

Tommy stood silently in the kitchen watching his chips through the glass section of the oven door.

"Next time you break a window you won't get any dinner." Kerry took Emma onto her knee and continued to watch the film. Tommy remained transfixed until the bell went 'ting' and his mother got up and came back into the kitchen. She put the food down on the table in front of him. He was silent as he ate and his eyes followed her about the room. He got up for the tomato sauce and squeezed a large blob onto his burger.

"He's so 'orrible. He won't do what I tell him. Last night he wet the bed again. Now he's broken the bedroom window. Five years old and wetting the bed! What's he going to be like in a few years' time?" Tommy munched on. His mother was speaking to his father. He didn't listen properly. He was fully focussed on his food. Kerry eventually replaced the receiver and went back to the screen. Then she lay Emma down just in front of the television and started to change her nappy, with one eye on the screen. Emma was compliant until Kerry tried to take the felt pen away, then she screamed. Tommy watched. Kerry let her daughter keep the pen but she put the top back on and tried to push it down hard. Emma immediately pulled it off and put it back in her mouth. Then his mother was putting more chips on his plate. He looked up at her with a little pleading glance, and picked up the tomato sauce. He was full but he didn't ever want to stop eating.

Kerry cuddled Emma and took her back to the settee to continue the film, but she had missed too much and could not understand the plot. Something had happened to do with a lump on the back of the heroine's head just below the hairline. She noticed Tommy was staring straight ahead at nothing, his mouth bulging with food. In fact, Tommy was revelling in his bulging mouth, the soft potato, the tangy sauce. He was sucking it, unwilling to let it go. He was in a daze.

"You stupid dreamy kid."

She turned quickly back. The film was gripping her again. The heroine was ill, possibly dying.

Tommy's glazed stare was towards the screen, but he wasn't seeing. His tummy felt full. His school trousers always had been too tight, now the waistband was giving way. A button had come off and it felt so good but he sensed it could mean trouble and pulled his shirt down. Kerry looked up and said.

"Pudding. That's what you want I expect."

Resentfully she rushed into the kitchen. If the heroine in the film died it would be the saddest of things, she was so beautiful and kind and had only just moved into this lovely house with a swimming pool. Kerry took the sponge pudding and treacle out of the can, topping it with a scoop of ice cream and a dollop of sweetened double cream. That would keep him quiet. Tommy experienced a retching sensation as he smelt the pudding, and then he started to eat. The woman was definitely dying. She was sitting waiting for the results of some blood tests. Her mouth fascinated Kerry. It was so soft looking, and bud-like. A doctor was saying it was a terminal illness. Kerry looked across and saw treacle trickling down Tommy's chin onto his uniform.

"Look at you! Just look at you! Your school uniform, stupid."

Emma stared at Tommy and gave a delighted gurgle. He caught her eye and pulled a face.

"I wish you'd never been born."

His mother spoke with her eyes on the screen but he didn't take in the words only the tone. He looked at the screen and saw a man gently stroking a woman's face.

Kerry glanced at her son. He looked pathetic. Stuffed with food. Humbled. On the verge of being sick. She picked up Emma kissing and hugging her until the toddler started giggling, helplessly.

Next door Vera and her husband were having their evening meal. They could hear Kerry's voice, raised now to furious shouting, "And look at your trousers, you're bursting out. Fat stupid pig."

"It's only mother talk. She's just worked up. No wonder if he's smashed the window." Len tried to speak with a matter-of-fact tone as he stirred his tea. He wished his wife didn't take so much notice. It was beginning to affect everything. What he wanted to do now was retire to the coast and get a dog. If you didn't give all your attention to such matters they didn't happen. For months now Vera had kept putting it off, yet it had always been a shared dream. They loved the coast, had many holidays there with their son, and years ago the three of them had laughed about what they called this 'vision for the future' their move down there, to the sea. Now the time had come. Time came, Len thought. That was the trouble, time had a way of coming and when it did it meant action.

"But you know what Gladys says about that little boy when he's at school." Gladys, his brother's wife, who worked at the school. His wife was continuing. "He cries a lot and doesn't want to run free in the playground."

"Well, we're not all gregarious."

"Then when they eventually get him to play... he doesn't really play... he runs around pushing other kids, not satisfied until one of them is screaming."

"Little blighter hey?

Vera looked across at her husband and tried to ignore her anxieties. She shouldn't rant on like this. He wanted peace. He'd worked hard at his factory job for 45 years. They'd both worked hard. Together they'd built a secure life and kept reasonably fit. Their one child had qualified as an engineer and lived in Canada. She asked, "What time shall we leave tomorrow?"

He looked up with a full mouth but his eyes brightened. They were off to the coast for three nights. She waited for him to swallow.

"There's three places to see."

"Yes, but that's the day after tomorrow. We needn't rush off too early in the morning."

It was always the same he thought, she had this strange reluctance to get away, yet once there she was happy as Larry.

"It's not what she says to the little chap, it's her tone. Like she scoffs. Not like scolding."

He didn't reply, thankful that they'd planned a few nights away. His wife needed a break.

*

Next morning Vera observed a man pass her window and concluded he was on his way to 'next door', most likely to do with the council. They were probably getting the message by now. Broken windows, school reports… Her quick glimpse took in a serious dark-skinned business-like man in a suit, walking quickly. He was probably a foreigner. The council had a lot of foreigners on their staff these days. The old lady on the other side had an African social worker. Wouldn't let her in at first, made a terrible fuss, but now she thought highly of her and wouldn't have a word said against her. What a relief. The council were in on it. Whatever was going wrong next door she could now keep out of it and let the authorities sort it out.

Kerry opened the door to Roberto. Early for him. He usually came late at night after the restaurant had closed. Always brief, to do with money. He came in and sat down. Abrupt. Tommy was at school and Emma was there with red stains all over her face. Roberto thought it was probably that healthy blackcurrant drink that the English children liked, but that kid wasn't his concern.

"You rang. You know I can't talk… at work."

He looked across at the television and then down at his watch. Kerry wondered how much money he had for her this time. He was already sitting down at the kitchen table, taking banknotes out of his wallet. As always it d everything, the counting.

"Like I said on the phone, Tommy is an awful bo

His response was to look up from his counting, his eyes dark, so dark, darker than Tommy's. To her he was just a man. There was nothing at all between them anymore. He could have been an insurance man or a central heating specialist, just making a house call.

"Tommy... bad boy sometimes..."

She thought his English had improved. He used to be so slow composing a reply. He continued counting.

"I can take you down to the school if you want to see Tommy."

He chose not to notice her tone and her feelings began to surface.

"Or perhaps you'd like to take him with you."

She had said this before and knew what the answer would be.

"You are the mother. I give you money."

"Please take him. I don't want him."

Her voice was oddly controlled and flat.

"No. No. I return to Italy... my mother is dying." He stood up. "I send you money still... always... always."

He stood up, preparing to leave.

She wasn't surprised at all by his attitude. This is how it had always been and yes, she felt sure he would keep sending money, but somehow that didn't mean anything. Not today. She needed something else, but not from him. Never from him.

She began to feel a bit glazed now as she watched him preparing to leave. Just a man in a suit with dark eyes and short legs.

"Okay. I go."

She wanted him to go but she heard herself saying.

"Do you see Luke?"

She was thinking perhaps, just perhaps, Roberto could talk to Luke about Emma... and...

"Luke?" he looked at her with a quizzical expression.

"Yes, you know Emma's father."

"Ah good man. His name not Luke. We tease him. Not really Luke. Luke his name in London. London Luke."

Roberto grinned and looked down.

"..iz Dereeee..k. Name proper. He left London. They went to New Zealand."

"They?"

"Yes. He had woman in h'ipswich. Teacher at small school."

He glanced at his watch.

"Work for me. Restaurant. Eleven thirty. Goodbye. Goodbye."

As he left he closed the door quietly, deliberately like he always did.

Vera noticed the man looked very tense as he walked past her window.

Kerry sat counting the notes. Six hundred and fifty pounds. That would certainly help if she had to pay Housing for the window. So that man Luke had left the restaurant. Always Luke for her. Roberto had just called him Derek but he knew exactly who she meant. After all he had introduced them. Emma's father. Not that she ever knew him. Not really. 'Luke.' She said the name aloud and had the usual reaction. Roberto and Luke had been friends working together at the restaurant. Tommy only little then. It had seemed odd because Roberto seemed to welcome, encourage even, his friend's interest in her. He actually introduced them. Even now it was nice thinking about Luke. When he came to the house that night, and he only came that once, she had found it impossible to escape his looks. It was like his looking at her did things, and undid things, and his manner was so gentle as if he was watching and looking out for her every need, like pouring her a glass of wine from the bottle he brought and putting it down so quietly, softly in front of her, his hand seeming to linger as if he wanted to leave it behind in her care. Such thoughts of him made her feel sexy even now, right down there below her stomach somewhere, and just a hint of that film yesterday floated back into her mind. That same sense of being engulfed, carried away, everything taken care of, everything safe. Safe but exciting.

She went to hide the money in an envelope in the wardrobe. It had never been like that with Roberto. She shuddered at the thought of their intimacy. His 'thing' had seemed so long and cumbersome. Sex had been like a kind of medical check at the Doctors. She was relieved to have nothing to do with it anymore, but Luke... he had been different. He had joked that his visit had been 'hello goodbye.' He had not mentioned Ipswich. It had only happened once but it was the only sex thing she had done that was nice remembering. She sat in a muddled daze puzzling whether Luke was his second name.

Vera was talking to Gladys on the phone. "The Council came yesterday."

"Not before time. That poor fat little boy. And he's getting fatter."

"What do you think they'll do?"

"Social Services?" Gladys sniffed importantly. "You never know. Probably nothing."

"But..."

"Then other times they zoom in and look at everything, quick smart. You know, come to the school and everything, us dinner ladies... talk, listen to what we have to say. Then they have a conference. Might put him on a register to do with protection... we've got three kids in care already at the school."

"You don't think they'd take him away from her?"

"They easily might. A lot depends on how they see the mother."

She put the receiver down and went back to the bedroom to continue packing. There'd been so much in the papers lately about bad things happening to children even when they were known by the authorities but it was time to stop thinking about all that. She told herself that the papers always published bad news. There was a letter from their son this morning, urging them to make the move to the coast. Do it before Christmas he said because I'm heading home then for ten days. Well, they were off to Hastings at four thirty. She was already deciding what she needed to take. They would be there for three nights and they were to look at flats with a view to exchanging and moving down there. At that moment she was strangely relieved to be going somewhere away from here, and yes she could see what Len wanted and she wanted it too. They could make it happen and they must.

When Kerry went to pick Tommy up, she felt ashamed of him. Fat. Unkempt. Wearing his tracksuit bottoms as his school trousers needed mending and anyway were much too small. She hurried away from the school pulling him along feeling not so much sleepy as dreamy. She needed to get home quickly. She had a video to watch that had to be back in the morning, and Emma was on her own. Little monkey that she was these days, she could be knocking things over and messing up the room. The other parents clustering around the school gate seemed familiar but strangely unreal, as if they were in a film which she didn't want any part in. They seemed to be watching her and she cursed Tommy under her breath. He was getting her a bad name. She tried to think about the cosmetics she needed. Her lipstick was down to its last stump. Her own face kept flashing before her as if in a mirror.

Back at the flats as she and Tommy got out of the lift, she was surprised to meet Mr and Mrs Hall waiting to get in, and with suitcases.

"Hello Tommy." Vera spoke without looking at Kerry, who was hanging on to her son to prevent him rushing at their neighbour and flinging his arms around her legs. Kerry looked at Len as he spoke.

"We're off at last."

He grinned and patted Tommy on the head as he drew his case into the lift.

"Bye mate."

The lift door closed, and Len put his case down and looked at Vera.

"Whew... she's an attractive girl that... it's a pity..." His voice trailed off. He thought Kerry was a fine looking young woman. Today her lipstick made her mouth look like one of those delicious iced coconut tarts with cherries.

Vera nodded. She respected her husband's comment, but really sometimes men didn't seem to see far below the surface. They couldn't seem to get out of the habit of looking first at a woman's figure and looks, and somehow confusing these with qualities of virtue.

Opening the door and going in with Tommy, Kerry felt miserable and less keen to get down to watching her latest film. The GP had recently told her it was not 'depression' when she got like this, she was just low and miserable. He would prescribe something to help her sleep and had she thought about joining a mother and toddler's group?

Tommy ran up to Emma who suddenly started to scream – he had trodden on her fingers, and it looked deliberate. Kerry pretended not to have seen. She didn't want a scene, she wanted to get settled with the new video. She comforted Emma and watched Tommy start to suck his way silently through two burgers and chips. The days when she made him remove his school clothes were long gone. It didn't even occur to her these days, and when she saw him beside the others at the school gates, she blamed him. He stood out. He was scruffy, fat and yuk. She put a large slice of cream and jam sponge cake with ice cream ready for his dessert. His eyes above the food seemed to mock at her, and plead with her, all at the same time. She sprinkled sugar on the ice cream. She wanted him quiet. So long as they both stayed quiet now. The video. She hugged Emma and settled her in cushions on the settee. Before pressing the forward button she addressed Tommy.

"Fat 'orrid pig. In the end no one will want you, Tommy."

She spoke quietly this time and spitefully, looking across at him over Emma's head. It seemed to upset him more than her raised voice. Large tears spilled from his eyes, and onto his plump pink cheeks. She repeated herself, quietly, looking straight at him. Then she returned to the screen.

Emma's eyes widened and suddenly she started to cry. Kerry hugged her but she would not be consoled. Then she started to scream and scream. The more Kerry tried to calm her the more she screamed. Pressing the pause button, Kerry looked at Tommy now, as if for help. His eyes were on her, and his mouth was full of food which he seemed reluctant to swallow. The screaming continued. She plonked the baby down on the floor and covered her ears, aware of a numbness, a sense of being isolated, invisible almost, with absolutely no influence on what was happening. It was all becoming unreal. Here in the flat she was slipping into emptiness where nothing mattered and she was powerless. She pressed the 'play' button. Onto the screen came a couple walking along a deserted golden beach, stopping from time to time to gaze into each other's eyes. Then the woman was running and laughing and the man caught her and they kissed, going to the ground with a sensual ease, as if their very actions would end everything and start everything all afresh. It was silent now as she stared at the screen.

Emma had stopped crying and Kerry became aware that she was making little gurgling noises of amusement. Her eyes left the screen and focussed on Tommy. He was pulling faces at his sister, and then she got up and toddled over to her brother at the table. The first time she had walked so far and confidently without support. He offered a spoonful of pudding. She accepted solemnly and opened her mouth wide for another. Kerry watched. Feeling nothing. Recognising nothing. The children, the screen, the objects in the room, they all seemed to be merging. Nothing was more real than anything else. She could no longer differentiate between the tears of the woman on the screen, who was now waving goodbye to the man as he drove away, and Tommy's tears still wet on his face as he clowned with Emma. The pattern on her rug and the well-spaced lines of flowers on the curtains seemed to be coming towards her, absorbing her, eating her up. She went upstairs for her temazepan, and emptied all the white tablets out onto the bed.

*

Vera and Len were now at Charing Cross Station ready for their departure to Hastings. She was now feeling quietly enthusiastic about this trip. Waves of optimism were gently washing across her mind and a sense of thankfulness prevailed. She looked at Len who was stirring his cappuccino and her thoughts went back to their flat and the lift, but then Tommy's eyes jerked into her mind and her mood changed. Her hand reached inside her handbag. Len suddenly became aware of his wife peering at her mobile, and then her voice.

"Is that you, Tommy? Get your mother for me."

He felt a glimmer of annoyance. Why wouldn't she let go? Then she gave a worried frown and thrust the phone towards him. In spite of the noise in the station forecourt he could hear Tommy's voice saying something like "...she won't wake up."

Then some odd snorting noises and a toddler almost screaming with delight, then Tommy's voice again, "She's sleeping... sleeping... sleeping..."

Len felt bewildered and handed the mobile back to his wife. She took it and began to dial. He looked around the station trying to calm himself. He'd go and get a newspaper in a minute. He needed to distance himself. His wife had it…she knew. Matter was urgent, dead urgent. His Vera was saying, "Is that the Social Services?"

Then she was spilling out all her worries about the neighbour and her kids. He felt a flood of relief and closed his eyes. On serious matters to do with that kid next door he was right behind her. Vera knew. Vera would be right. She was one woman in a million.

They were listening and asking questions.

"I believe she's unconscious and in charge of two kids."

He listened. They listened. Vera went on. She was going in the right direction. It was time his wife offloaded onto the people who were paid to do the job. He could see the relief in her face as well as still some concern as she turned towards him.

"That was the man on duty in the child protection section. They're doing an urgent visit with the police."

"Well done, love. They'll deal with it now."

She put her mobile in her bag and zipped it methodically.

Charing Cross was buzzing. Now, what was that announcement? He thought it was an accent with an Afro-Caribbean flavour. The way those chaps talked you got the feeling there was a party going on in the background. Ah yes, he could understand it now. It was platform 8 to Hastings. He touched her shoulder and their eyes met. There was a lot that couldn't be in their marriage after all these years but the camaraderie was stronger than it had ever been.

Dinner Party: Two

Cyril: Would you like some lovely dessert wine? It's special.

Susan: Just a drop.

Tom: And for me please.

All: Cheers.

CLINK OF GLASSES

Cyril: We had some real upsets in our street yesterday. Police, ambulance, the lot…

Susan: Oh really. What was all that about?

Cyril: Young woman overdosed and with two kids.

Kathy: Cyril, don't worry our guests with all that.

Susan: Gosh. Sounds awful… and two children… yes, drop more thanks.

Kathy: Well we're not sure of the outcome are we, Cyril? It could be… er… really, really serious.

Cyril: No. Don't think so. She's probably in hospital now enjoying a three-course dinner.

Susan: Let's hope so. Hmm… this wine is superb. What happened to the kids?

Cyril: God only knows.

Tom: But does he, Cyril?

Kathy: They went off in a car, something to do with the council.

Susan: Ah, Kathy. This dessert looks absolutely delicious.

Cyril: Yes. My wife is an amazing cook. What I want to know, is why young people aren't more self-disciplined.

Tom: Self-discipline. What's that, Cyril?

Cyril: It means you don't always do what you want, when you want. You ask yourself. Now is this sensible? It's as simple as that. Common sense.

Susan: Oh, I see... Mmm lovely wine.

Kathy: Well perhaps I should say... after all we *are* all in this together. I did hear the woman died before they got her to hospital.

Susan: Oh God!

SILENCE

Cyril: Extra large slice for me, Kathy.

Kathy: Cyril darling, you know you've been warned about your weight. You mustn't overeat. Don't want to end up in hospital again.

Cyril: Rubbish, dear wife. Large slice please and a good dollop of double cream.

Fly Me To The Moon

The sunlight was streaming through the front door as she came downstairs that morning, the coloured glass making a kind of theatrical rainbow. Not true rainbow colours but the impact was just as encouraging after the grey, dismal days of the last few weeks.

She sat for a moment on the lounge settee and listened to her father pottering in the kitchen. He would be trying to make tea. He would be putting the tea bags in the milk and emptying the contents of the jug into the electric kettle. Her intuition was to let him try. After a long pause, which was usual while he waited for it to brew, he began to walk slowly through the hall.

"Morning Dad."

He was concentrating on balancing the tray with two cups full of weak-looking liquid with bits of tea bag floating on top. With each step the liquid slopped into the saucers. He didn't say anything

"First cup of the day time?"

She jumped up as she spoke, telling herself not to rush at him. It only upset him when he could see she was exasperated. She must let him do things in his own time. Taking his arm, she turned him back towards the kitchen. It was the regular morning pattern.

"Norma likes it strong first thing."

"The stronger the better I imagine." Diane beat him to his usual comment.

"She's having a little lie-in." He spoke more to himself now than to his daughter.

Diane glanced through the hatch into the dining room where her mother's ashes were in their container on the mantelpiece.

"Yes. Quite a long one. Er... I'll make a pot."

He settled himself down in a chair at the kitchen table.

"It's a change this sunshine."

He didn't reply. She whisked the tray away and emptied the unappetising looking drinks into the sink, rinsed out the electric kettle and started again He waited. He was always willing to sit and wait once she was busy with a task related to him. It was unnerving the way he had become so dependent. For someone like her, first denying herself children, and then later a dog, and later still even a cat, it had at times a bitter edge No matter how much you guarded your freedom, or how many sacrifices you made in order to remain free, there was no guarantee. Life had a way of suddenly pinning you down.

"I was singing last night, Dad. The 606 Club." She never gave up talking to him as if he understood, and sometimes she thought he did, but he rarely replied. The gig last night had gone well, and this morning she was in good spirits. She had been offered two jazz bookings at the Edinburgh Festival next year.

"Did it wake you when I came in?" He didn't reply, he was up, going for another cup, as she poured tea into two clean mugs on the table.

"No Dad. Two's enough. There's just us. You and me."

She stressed the 'you' and 'me'. He ignored her and put a clean cup down, a trifle annoyed. Should she humour him and pour one for his dead wife? She was as always at a loss to know.

"Okay. One for Norma." She could handle it as 'for Norma' but not as 'for mother'.

"She likes..."

"Yes. It strong, first thing."

He watched as she poured into the cup. He always got a cup, rather than a mug, for his wife, and in that respect his memory was serving him well. The fact that he forgot the saucer would soon have been checked by her mother.

He was still a large handsome man, and although a bit stooped had long legs, slim broad shoulders, a muscular back, and this morning was wearing smart trousers over his pyjamas. Incongruous really, as he had become so childlike and vulnerable. Naughty as well, like the other day in the chemist shop when he wouldn't put the scented condoms back and she had to purchase them. Now what on earth had made him do that? Later in his room she found he'd put condoms over all the miniature lighthouses in her mother's collection in the bedroom. Sometimes you had to smile.

Undoubtedly he was getting worse. Even leaving him alone, like last night, she'd actually locked him inside which was wrong. It was all worrying, although once on the job she had felt better. Singing got things out of her system. 'Mack the knife.' 'Just one of those things.' 'Fly me to the moon.' Hushed room. Her voice. The musicians playing. The audience. Applause. Everything else in her life momentarily suspended. After her mother died her father was okay for the first year then his Alzheimer's set in. Gently at first and he joked about it. Came into city centre several times to hear her sing. Ronnie Scotts, Pizza Express, Purcell Room. She recalled how one night after the event he got on the wrong train and finished up at Margate. Not that that was so bad, her friend had done that once. But he phoned and was clearly confused. Thought he was in Brighton looking for a hotel he had booked for a holiday and asking where was the pier and then going on about the Germans, they hadn't left a trace when they'd bombed the Pavilion…

"I've put your clothes out on the bed, Dad."

This morning her good spirits were persisting and she could be, as she liked to be, loving, tolerant, patient. Not always like this. Other times she was irritable with him, appalled by his decline.

"Hey Dad. 'How deep is the ocean?' I sang it."

He gave one of his quick little looks that could have meant anything, but she liked to interpret it as 'heard and understood.' He put the cup on the tray with his half finished mug and moved into the hall on his way upstairs with his wife's tea.

"Dad. I sang your song."

"Norma's a complicated woman. Very, very deep." He was muttering to himself but turned as he spoke and the mug slipped on the tray and fell onto the hall carpet.

"Dad! You are so…"

She rushed into the hall and began mopping up the liquid with kitchen roll and taking the tray from him. He pottered on through the hall making his way upstairs seemingly unaffected. She spoke to herself suddenly near to tears.

"So… so… so sweet."

He was so endearing at times. She wanted only to put her arms around him and hold him close and guarantee him all that felt good and enhanced his well being. He must have no distress. No humiliation. No pain. She wanted to sing, to comfort him, to put everything right, but instead she returned to the kitchen for more cleaning utensils.

So long as she could sing, be asked to sing, earn her keep. It had been a fight to stay adrift in a world of television X factors and celebrity promoting agents. When she didn't get contracts, reality was always there waiting, snarling at her like a large angry dog, that needed to be handled, placated. How to keep the high standard of her singing voice, how not to take any job which ate into her practice sessions. How to be poor and proud, deprived of fame and glamour but not bitter. How big was her heart? Was her faith blind? And now she had this unexpected threat, lurking ominously some days, other times sleepy, non threatening, lovable, compliant.

"Be careful on the stairs."

She yelled out suddenly from the kitchen. The other day he had tripped on the laces of one of his trainers, and fallen on rather than down the stairs. Nothing wrong with his body, it was his brain. The way it instructed his body parts. It was making her nervous too. She would soon be in her fifties. Sometimes she worried that there were annoying smudges and shifts occurring in her own memory. Store this, keep that on board, put this in a place ready for quick reliable response. Seeing her father's mind making him like he had become was alarming. He had been a very competent surveyor, well thought of by many.

Inevitably now she thought of Simon as he zoomed into her mind from somewhere underneath where he always waited. The other man in her life who would not seem to go away. Still occasionally her pianist but in the past so much more than her pianist. Those hands, so alive, intelligent, sensitive. The way he accompanied her singing. Watchful, responsive, so fully focussed. What a backer he'd been. Until all the trouble developed with her scat singing.

Ah, the doorbell. It would be Ted. One of her father's friends. Loyal friend. His most loyal. He had come to say he would be back later this afternoon to 'sit George' so she could go shopping. George and Ted had known each other since they were both surveyors in a local firm. Ted was small with a bright gritty smile and he walked with difficulty using a stick, sometimes two sticks. He seemed to have become smaller and thinner as he aged, but his brain was as good as ever. It found unusual ways of compensating for his failing limbs.

"How's he then, today?"

"Just the same... silly old Dad."

Ted noticed the tears in her eyes and thought how George would have hated being reliant on his daughter like this. Just as well he was in cloud cuckoo land.

"You're going to have to do some serious thinking." His tone was stern. Ted didn't think she should have to give up her singing career. Singing was her life, and Norma and George had had a lot to do with that. They hadn't exactly been pushy parents but they had been very excited when her singing got recognition. It was somehow out of the realm of all the usual stepping stones parents craved, it had been a source of amazement and wonder. He'd seen it all, and he didn't underestimate music himself either, even if whistling was his sole contribution. He smiled inwardly to himself.

"Yes, Yes. I'm trying, Ted. Someone's coming from social services later this morning."

"See you at three then."

He turned in his familiar careful way and began to focus on the complicated processes of walking back up the path and onto the pavement to his parked car. As he did he remembered the bad times as well when Diane and her man had fought bitterly in front of Norma and George. Simon was a brilliant pianist. A very steady man too. Reliable. Supportive. Well educated. Diane had been a handful. Shaking his head he negotiated the curb and unlocked his car. His legs were going well today, must be the sun.

*

Diane went up to change the under sheet on her father's bed. It had been going on for a couple of months now, the bedwetting. First discovering the wet mattress and bedclothes had been upsetting, but regularly now he lay in bed thinking he was already standing at the toilet. Extraordinary the way he sat in the bedroom and watched her remaking the bed. She needed help with her father. Basically that was it. The phone rang again half way through her task. It was the accompanist from the gig last night. He was enquiring about her availability for more work north of Edinburgh after the festival.

Her father was making his way downstairs, as she replaced the receiver, looking quite dapper.

"No Dad. Don't go out. You don't go to work anymore. Ted is coming later."

How many times had she explained to him. He was retired. He didn't work. Today she didn't attempt to reason with him but coaxed him into the kitchen and he sat down while she put on boiled eggs for them both. As usual, she noticed with chagrin, he would stay around while she was doing something, preparing something for him, but as soon as she turned her attention elsewhere he became restless. If she hadn't have known that in the past he had been an independent and thoughtful man, she would have suspected him of being stubborn and seeking to be the centre of attention.

The woman from the council turned up right on time. Diane didn't know what to expect from a social worker, never having had to consult one until now. What she had picked up from the media was a bit off-putting. She anticipated a non-judgemental vagueness and little direction. No real help. She told George numerous times that someone was coming to see him, but he paid no attention and busied himself moving the indoor plants from one room to another.

The social worker turned up in a bright yellow Fiat Punto and was dressed in a smart trouser suit with a cream blouse. Diane glimpsed the photo on the identity card she flashed at the door. Her, yes, a likeness, but a good ten years ago, Diane thought, as she invited her in and went to look for her father who was upstairs in his bedroom taking the condoms on and off the lighthouses. The social worker looked at Diane and saw a large shapely mouth, a hint of nicotine stain on the teeth, a face which nicely combined youth with the gentle onset of middle age.

They sat in the lounge with George and talked. The woman was okay, she listened to Diane and then spoke directly to George. Diane was relieved. It seemed they were getting straight to the root of the problem. George was telling the woman that he lived with his sister, who did his washing and collected his pension. He thought it was Kent where he lived. It was lovely living here in the country. Those crowded London suburbs. He wouldn't want to live there anymore. Oh no.

The social worker persisted.

"But this is Greenwich. Not Kent."

"Oh no. No it's not. Kent is the garden of England... I like living here."

"So, your sister. Is she with us now? I mean, in this room?"

The woman looked directly at George and gestured towards Diane.

There was a pause.

"Is this your sister?"

George looked towards Diane, smiled and nodded.

"Is this your sister?"

The social worker persisted.

"Yes. Yes. That's her. My big sister. Bullies me on the school bus." George spoke now without conviction as if he was beginning to find it all trivial. He had struggled with this visitor long enough and he switched on the TV and ignored them, back in his own world with no sense whatsoever of what was being discussed. Diane looked at the social worker and found herself becoming tearful as she enquired.

"What can you do?"

"I'll do what I can. I can see he's going to be increasingly at risk And you must be able to continue your work. Not a good idea, as you have said, to lock him in at night."

"Yes... I must, I mean continue to work, and no I'm not going to lock him in anymore. Haven't told anyone but you. I've made an awful mess of some things."

On the verge of tears she sniffed and shook her head, adding, "Sorry. Sorry. I don't mean Dad. I haven't made a mess of that..." This was ridiculous. The woman was here about her father.

"No. But I can see the problem. I'll have to speak with the medical people..." The woman's voice was quiet but firm. Diane sipped her coffee.

"Do you have brothers or sisters?"

"Oh no. Only child... and I have no children. Divorced. An amicable divorce." Amicable. Now why had she said that? It was not quite the word. Well. It was more than 'not quite', it was wrong, very wrong.

"I mean… I should say it wasn't amicable, it was painful… took a long time to… left me empty."

The Social worker nodded, she was used to these previously painful memories crowding in at times like this. Diane closed her eyes and shook her head. What was she saying? She hadn't felt empty for ages. She used to feel empty, but… Why all this now?

"I'll do what I can. It seems to me your father needs residential care, but we can't always get this straight away."

The woman left, already preoccupied with all the procedure now necessary. The facts would have to be presented officially to a panel who would question everything. She smiled quietly to herself as she settled back in her car and quickly wrote down a few main points.

Diane made herself another strong coffee. Ridiculous. Why had she brought up her marriage. Of course she regretted the divorce, the quarrels… her fault, her fault, so much of it. His voice came to her, 'You are too adventurous, I agree it worked but you can't always expect spontaneity.' Her pianist, husband for one year only. She still heard this conversation when she was distressed, and her own voice 'What do you mean, you can't expect? I do expect? I want you always to respond.'

'It's scat singing, Diane, and when I don't know what you're going to do next.'

'Simon, you have to respond. Improvise. Like today. You improvised so well.'

'It would have been helpful to know the possible rhythm changes, how and when you were going to end it.'

A long silence as she slid away from him to her side of the bed.

'Darling. There has to be some planning even if it's for flexibility on the night.'

'No Simon. It has to be spontaneous. A move of the moment. A now sound.'

'Then I can't always guarantee a response.'

'That's because you should have gone down the classical route.'

'Diane, you're being impossible. I love improvisation but I must have an idea of tune and rhythm changes and the words... I had no idea you were going to sing those words.'

'Well it worked.'

'Yes it did. Very well, but my point is I need some idea. I'm only suggesting a rough plan within which you can...'

'Leave it, Simon. That is not my intention.'

Why, why. She needn't have made this such an issue. It had eaten into their life together, their work life, social life, sex life. Her scream for spontaneity. His for flexible planning.

She could hear her father in the kitchen. He always knew when it was time for a meal. Never had to be called. It was disturbing to her the way he ate, without any interest in what he was eating but as if he was ravenous. He had been a very discriminating eater. He'd always had wine with his main meal. Now he drank Ribena or Lucozade.

She went through to the kitchen and gave him his lunch. As she turned to make herself a sandwich she felt things shifting and sliding in her mind and had a momentary sense of clarity about where she stood in relation to her father. The social worker had done a thorough look around the house, even the lighthouses. Diane couldn't help smiling and began to feel more positive. She moved to the dining room with her sandwich, looking towards the casket on the mantelpiece. Her mother had encouraged her to sing, told her how much pleasure her singing brought to them and others, and more than that, the importance of improving her voice, always working to improve, striving for artistic heights. She was going to keep it up. She would phone the accompanist and make sure she got this work after the festival. She began to hum softly to herself, to hear the double bass and then the piano. Her voice made its way into the music, with a touch of harmony, a jibe, a humorous improvisation, and then she was in singing straight and clear, but swinging like a bird flying jubilantly, migrating to a land far away where the sun shone and the pleasures were of body, mind and soul. All focussed like that, no in between. No ordinary. When she finished, her father was standing at the door. And then, to her absolute surprise, he started to clap.

*

Ted arrived on time. He had brought some dominoes and some cans of beer. Very occasionally George had one but he never finished it, and it wasn't recommended on his medication. Diane had the view that just the smell of it made him feel good. Of course, he could no longer play dominoes but Ted persisted and had devised an easy but meaningless game in which one talked and put a domino down and then the other had a turn. This at least got George to stay in one place. He would sit at this, making nonsense conversation, and then playing his domino. He often chuckled at some point and looked away. Ted would swear at him as the game progressed. The restlessness would seem to subside, the smell and sight of the beer and dominoes drawing him back to the old patterns and rhythms of the past.

When Diane returned from the supermarket Ted said there had been a phone call for her about work. When she dialled the number she found it was an agent, who was absent at the moment. His secretary wasn't sure what he wanted but would tell him Diane was now at home.

She joined George and Ted, as she often did, and waited for her turn to put a domino down. Before that, the phone rang. Ted observed her taut condition and thought it was something to do with a singing contract. He'd seen it all before.

"Is that Diane Ferguson? Mel Edwards here. I have an offer to make. Looking for a singer to join a cruise liner in the Caribbean... special cruise, music all jazz, top class stuff. Passengers will come with high expectations. No commercial nonsense. Your name put forward..."

She thought 'wow' to herself and asked questions. She'd turned cruises down in the past because they usually asked for a more commercial style, but this one sounded perfect and somebody had recommended her... Caribbean. For two months. Promise of other work to follow.

"I don't want a too speedy decision. Take a few hours to consider. And make sure."

She sat down at the table and took up her dominoes. When her turn came she told of the offer. Ted nodded and grinned. His look made her feel she was as good as gone. Her father put down his dominoes and stared at Ted. They all laughed and Diane wished it was as simple as all that. Then her father got up and started looking for Norma. He was particularly clumsy and knocked over a chair. He could be heard in the kitchen opening the fridge door. There was a smash as a casserole dish hit the tiled floor.

*

The next day a letter came from social services saying that medical checks were being made and residential care considered. Respite care in a local home could start within two weeks and the placement, if approved, would become permanent. Family could go and look over the home before deciding. Diane nodded seriously to herself after reading the letter. That would work, could work, almost certainly would work, but then again it might not.

She was needed on board in four weeks. Visas and medical checks would be necessary but would her father be settled? True. Things rarely worked in perfect harmony. There could be problems but you couldn't stay at home because to do otherwise would have some risks. Weigh up the risks. Decide. She reread the letter. Timing was always going to be a tricky matter. Musicians knew that… especially pianists. She smiled to herself. If she didn't go for this she might never get another chance.

'Let's do some practice sessions together to prepare for your scatting.' Simon's voice when they were booked for an outdoor festival event.

'No. No. It's gotta be on the hoof.'

'Don't bring horses into this.'

'Simon. Be serious.'

'I am serious. So serious I actually looked scatting up in the Oxford Dictionary. Talking of horses it's something to do with another animal. Cats. You know, shooing cats off, hissing, sss…cat!'

'Look you might find it funny. I don't.'

So that was it. Eventually her good man was lost. That's life. That's music. More importantly now she was taking this work. Ted would back her all the way.

*

Very late that night when George was in bed, Diane started to go over in her mind the various items of clothes she would need for her work on the liner. The more she planned and became convinced that she was going, the more her feelings for her father flooded out of her in the form of tears, but her resolve to go never faltered. She was going for him as well as herself and her mother.

When next day she told of her preparations during dominoes, and of the care plan for George to be taken gradually into local residential care, Ted listened and nodded in agreement. He knew it would be a local care home and he would be able to visit, just like now. The game would go on. He enjoyed it as much as George. When Diane put down her next domino George sat back and looked at her, then he smiled. His old, quiet, warm smile. Had he understood? He signalled to her to put out her hand and pressed a domino into her clutches. She sat clasping this domino, her eyes wandering from her father to Ted. It was the double six.

When she checked her emails all the conditions of the project were made clear. Copy sign and return. Then a message to open. Diane stared in disbelief. Simon Latimer. He had put her name forward. She read 'Looking forward to our project. Want to take you on again, scatting or otherwise. I've been working on my flexibility.'

She reread it and knew. Divorce or not, they were on again. Sometimes sadness made joy more subtle, more poignant. Can you plan for spontaneity? Perhaps not.

About the author

The author was born on a farm in Lincolnshire. She completed an intensive four year course at Sydney University qualifying with a degree in social science and a social work diploma, after which she worked in prisons as a parole officer in New South Wales, and later in other areas of social work in the UK.

She now lives in the Royal Borough of Greenwich.